THE AUTHOR

Edith Templeton was born in Prague in 1916, in the last years of the Austro-Hungarian Empire. Both sides of her family were big estate owners in Bohemia – with the coming of communism, the castle, hung with magnificent tapestries, where she was brought up was turned into a museum. Edith was educated at the French Lycée and then at the Prague Medical University for three years and, after several short stays in England, she settled, at the age of twenty-two, first in Cheltenham and then in London. She married Dr Edmund Ronald, for twenty years a brilliant cardiologist in India, physician to the King of Nepal, first European to enter its royal palace, and *éminence grise* in that country. While with him in Calcutta, she met Nehru, the Dalai Lama and the Panchen Lama and, of course, quite a few maharajahs. She has since lived, apart from her first four years in Vienna and afterwards her native city, in Salzburg, Lausanne, Torremolinos, Estoril and Italy. During the war she worked for the American War Office, in the office of the Surgeon General, and from 1945-6 was a captain with the British Forces in Germany as conference and law court interpreter.

Although she started writing at the age of four – her first story being published when she was ten – Edith Templeton's first novel, *Summer in the Country*, was not published until 1950. Its success was followed by *Living on Yesterday* (1951) and *The Island of Desire* (1952) – all three are published by The Hogarth Press. She is also the author of several other volumes, including a travel book, *The Surprise of Cremona*, as well as many short stories and magazine articles, having been a regular contributor to the likes of *Vogue*, *Harpers* and the *New Yorker*. She has one son and now lives in Bordighera, on the Italian Riviera.

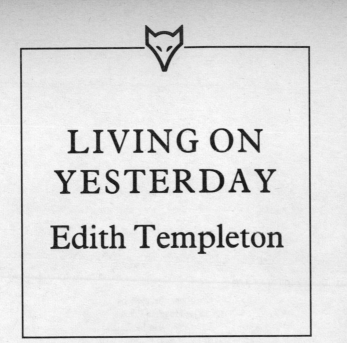

LIVING ON YESTERDAY

Edith Templeton

New Introduction by
Anita Brookner

THE HOGARTH PRESS
LONDON

Published in 1986 by
The Hogarth Press
Chatto & Windus Ltd
40 William IV Street, London WC2N 4DF

First published in Great Britain by Eyre and Spottiswoode Ltd 1951
Hogarth edition offset from the original British edition
Copyright Etta Trust Reg., Vaduz
Introduction copyright © Anita Brookner 1986

British Library Cataloguing in Publication Data

Templeton, Edith
Living on Yesterday
I. Title
823'.914[F]   PR6070.E4 /

ISBN 0 7012 0721 3

Printed in Great Britain by
Cox & Wyman Ltd
Reading, Berkshire

INTRODUCTION

It is perhaps necessary from time to time to remind the English reader that Bohemia is a geographical and social entity and not merely a province ruled over by Virginia Woolf. Edith Templeton, born in Prague, writes in exile from her native land with a biting economy and reticence alarmingly at odds with the home-grown kindliness of her English contemporaries. *Living on Yesterday*, published in 1951, was her second novel; it made good the promise of *Summer in the Country* and prepared the way for the dark complexities of *The Island of Desire*. It was valiantly received by the critics, who recognised an outstanding talent; its disquieting messages, which seemed to come from an older country and a more bitter code of social behaviour, were, as ever, graciously welcomed into an English context. The writer, was, implicitly, invited to feel at home. But in order to feel at home in England, it is necessary to entertain the English and not to frighten them. It is Edith Templeton's triumph that she manages to be superbly entertaining while casting her Bohemian eye over the elaborate stratagems of social advancement and regression which have always occupied her and which are in themselves rather frightening. During her many exiles from her native land she has never ceased to write about Prague, its sophistications and its beautifully managed misdemeanours. She writes impeccable English but she is a resolutely un-English writer, and in her taut and clever novels she encapsulates a tradition that is alien, expansive, and unsettling.

Less sentimental than Schnitzler, less heavy-handed than Fontane, less determinist than Jean Rhys – all of whom she greatly admires – Edith Templeton possesses the knowledge that our successes are achieved by the skin of our teeth and our failures will cost us dear. Always. It is up to each of us to save our own lives, which is what Hedwig and Ferdinand do in *Living on Yesterday*. Both are presented as too good to be true. Hedy is the repressed and obedient daughter of the immensely rich Baron Kreslov; Ferdinand, Count Szalay, is the elegant veteran of a Hungarian cavalry regiment. To Hedwig's mother, Baroness Kreslov, the two are obviously made for each other; all that she requires is a little help with the introductions. So what could be simpler than for her to give a small party to bring them together? Except that this is an afternoon reception, from five to eight, with all the ground floor rooms open *en enfilade*, and a master chef to supervise the buffet, which ranges from caviar to Russian eggs, from salmon to carp, from smoked ham to veal slices interleaved with *foie gras*, from vanilla custards with chocolate sauce to hazelnut ice cream, from glacé fruits to 'monumental' cakes. Clearly these people are different from us.

There is something odd about Count Szalay, but it turns out that there is something odd about Hedwig Kreslov as well. They are indeed made for each other. Whether or not the alliance is a misalliance is the subject of the book. But certain characters are there to shed an oblique light on this very intriguing matter. There is the immensely resourceful Steffanie Smejkal, fading beauty, ex-mistress of a prince, wearing her impeccable black dress, into the belt of which she has tucked her long gloves, and her black velvet hat with its trembling aigrette of osprey feathers. There is Richard Marek, Baroness Kreslov's brother, a rough-mannered man but with an infallible sense of social duties and requirements. There are humorous, resigned husbands who watch their wives' machinations with a sense of what it is going to cost them. There is an old retainer who is quick to spot an error. There is a radiantly insensitive business man from Pardubice who never gets his manners quite right. All these characters, except the last, are superbly confident of their place in society, a society alert to the slightest infringement of its rules. And beneath the elaborate superficialities of such a society there runs a sense of authenticity, of worth properly judged. 'He looks like a man,' says Steffanie Smejkal at one point. 'And because he looks like one he thinks he is one.' No judgement could be simpler or more profound.

The yesterday of the title is, of course, illusory, the past to which we all lay claim with a mixture of fantasy and regret. It is today that pays the bills, and it is today that the bills must be paid. The Baroness and the Count are quite in agreement on this point. Methods of payment vary according to status, but society demands that all transactions must be covered by good manners. Edith Templeton does not tear a passion to tatters. She conveys it in precise and well-tailored sentences of aphoristic brevity. The intimacy of Hedwig and Ferdinand and of their married life is never even hinted at, but their complicity is manifest. Money has united them, money has changed their destinies, and money, as is well known, and as is clearly acknowledged here, can arouse very strong passions. The urbanity with which the passionate importance of money is handled is perhaps the clearest evidence that we are dealing with a very old society indeed. 'Only connect' may be an essentially bourgeois command; here the connection is clearly understood as financial.

These rich and not so rich people, all of whom manage to live so well, are drilled and mannered down to their every glance. The dreadful Baroness Kreslov, so dreadful that her relations marry unsuitably just in order to annoy her, is a controlled and worldly woman who never gives overt offence. Her daughters think of disobedience in the schoolroom but are always well behaved in the salon. Steffanie Smejkal did not pass her youth at court for nothing. Count Szalay is a very model of elegance and refinement, both apparent and real. The Baroness's volatile brother, Richard Marek, is undeniably a gentleman. The homely providers of the money that makes the wheels go round are tactful enough never to labour the point. Even the servants are devoted to their duties and the households proceed with a voluptuous efficiency which will strike the harassed contemporary reader as both extraordinary and sublime. Although the novel was published only thirty years ago it tells of a society that has utterly vanished: that is a cliché, but one which is in this instance only too true. The upper bourgeoisie of Edith Templeton's memory is a baroque society, saved from decadence by its superb sense of style. Her characters are, in their own way, stoics.

Edith Templeton's own style has something stoical about it, and she shares the perfect manners of her characters. 'How do you live?' the reader is entitled to ask of these people. This is how they live. '[They] were served with mushroom omelette, grilled pike with a sour egg-sauce, hot ham with spinach and Madeira sauce, chestnut pudding with cream, and Gruyère cheese with red pepper fried on triangle of white bread.' This is the food of memory, elaborate, abrupt, and specific. It is also a gracious prologue, after which negotiations can take place: the prospective son-in-law has been shown the tenor of the house. And the quality of Edith Templeton's exile is evident not only in her patient sophistication but in sudden memories as precise as an hallucination. 'They skirted the clearing. A small stone bridge spanned a ravine full of stones, twigs, and bracken. Brambles, elders, and hazelnuts rustled against the horses' flanks and parted and closed with a hissing sound like tearing silk. Stripling oaks grew among grassy boulders, and above the thorny, sombre, and untidy undergrowth, the checkered stems of birch trees rose thin, clear, and smooth against the delicate blue sky.' This is a momentary glimpse in the course of a significant dialogue, and it gives that dialogue a legendary charm. With the elements so favourable, surely the ending must be a happy one? And so it is, but not in the way anticipated by the reader.

It is necessary to be brave in order to sympathise fully with these characters, who are so brave themselves. Adventurers with perfect manners are rather rare in our society, and many of us tend to behave as if we were excused the full responsibility for our actions. To be steely, wary, and overwhelmingly charming is, of course, rather difficult, and it takes an enormous amount of talent. The breathtaking Mrs. Kalny, of *The Island of Desire*, is proof of that, and it is perhaps *The Island of Desire* that marks Edith Templeton's apogée as an historian of manners. But *Living on Yesterday* is her most perfect novel, both from the point of view of observation and of form. It is a novel that should be recognised for what it is: a most honourable exercise in the European tradition, and a classic of its kind.

Anita Brookner, London 1985

CHAPTER 1

THE BARONESS KRESLOV had just taken off one glove and was unfastening the buttons of the other, when the noise started overhead.

A step behind her stood Joseph, slightly bent forward, with his right arm curved deferentially in readiness to receive her furs, and with his left arm pressed to the satin braid of his trousers.

Neither of them made the faintest move, and thus they remained for the next few seconds, while a man's voice shouted words which they could not distinguish, alternating with dull and heavy thuds. When a door on the landing above the stairs flew open and books were flung over the banisters and tumbled down the steps, they did not raise their eyes. The sound of a violent scuffle followed, the door slammed and then the tall clock in the hall got ready to strike. There issued a whirring of wheels, the hammer creaked and three faint and metallic booms announced the hour.

The Baroness straightened herself and buttoned up her gloves again. 'Three o'clock already, I did not think it was so late.'

'The clock is a bit fast, madam.'

7

'Even so, Joseph.' And she took a step forward and looked up. In front of the now closed and silent door sat a brown spaniel, gazing ahead of him with grief and dignity, all the more touching as he had never squealed while being kicked out by his master. The books – there were only two, although they had seemed to be much more numerous only a few moments ago – rested almost in front of the Baroness's feet, one of them suspended from a tread like a white fan.

'I don't think I will stay, Joseph. As I said before, I did not realize it was so late. Tell my brother I called, will you?' And with those words the Baroness made her way to the door with that slow and purposeful gait which was peculiar to her.

Following behind her, Joseph murmured: 'The master will be sorry when he hears——'

'I don't think he is quite in the mood for visitors. It was nothing important, anyway.'

Her voice was low and firm; she moved her shoulders with a decisive gesture, to settle the fur round her throat, and held herself more upright than ever. And as she turned round presently to face the servant, she looked exactly as she intended to look: tall and unevenly grey-haired, fresh skinned and with commanding, somewhat bulging blue eyes, the heavy mature bosom thrust out by her attitude, adding an air of motherly dignity: the picture of a well-bred matron who was used to nothing but respect from all the world and who had decided to postpone her call because of the advanced time of the day and for no other reason.

Glancing beyond his head, she contemplated the small drawing-room situated at the back of the hall, whose doors had been thrown apart. The shining ebony of the grand piano reflected the sky-blue of velvet hangings and the glitter of gilt frames.

'You should have the blinds down on a day like this,' she said. 'Every colour fades, but blue most of all. An awkward colour; I always said so. One fine day you will draw the curtains and find that they will be all patchy. And what will you do then? In Bubenc that will never happen.'

Bubenc was the part of the town where the Baroness lived. And when she said 'Bubenc', she did not mean that every householder in that district protected his curtains from the sun; she referred to her own house and to her own house only. In the same manner she spoke of 'the grand-parents' and 'the parents', meaning her own family, just as one speaks of 'the sun' and 'the moon', the sole existing planets of their kind.

'The master does not like the blinds drawn, madam,' replied Joseph and he closed his mouth and breathed carefully through his nose, a habit of his when he was on his guard.

'It is not a case of liking or not liking, I should have thought. In questions like these one has to pocket one's prejudices.'

'It's just that he does not want the house to look mournful, madam. It's ever since – once and never again, he said to me at the time. If it was not doctors, it was nurses; and if it was not nurses, it was priests. All the comings and goings, it was more than he could stand.'

The Baroness turned on her heels after a last look of pain and disapproval at the drawing-room. She walked across the well-polished parquet floor inlaid with stars and lozenges of coloured woods, past the clock and the yellow Venetian

9

chairs, with Joseph following at a respectful distance of three steps. Then, as she reached the flower stand and the hall table whose marble top was supported by the intertwined arms of three marble figures, and where the salver for cards reposed between a brush with yellowed bristles, a broken comb and an embossed brass bell, he came quickly forward and opened the door for her. She went out with an absentminded nod of the head and on the pavement she stopped and smoothed her black kid gloves. She began to walk and, passing the last window of her brother's house, she lifted her chin and raised her eyes to the sky, with a well-simulated expression of amazement and resignation. Then, looking in front of her, where the steeply sloping street led into the main square of the town, with two sluggish streams of trams, cars and people rolling in opposite directions, she composed her features.

A warm wind swept whirls of dust over the uneven pavement and forced her to close her eyes from time to time. She reached the city museum, a gloomy stone building which no one ever visited, and turned into a quiet side street where she knew her car to be waiting.

CHAPTER 2

'HERE ARE the books you mislaid, sir.' Joseph stopped by the door and bent his head, so that the grizzled strip of beard which ran from his temples to his cheeks almost touched his collar, while the lower part of his peasant face was hidden in the folds of the white neckcloth which gave some distinction to his shabby livery.

Richard Marek, standing in front of his desk, emitted a sound which could have been taken for a sigh or for a snort. Joseph could not distinguish his master's expression, as his face was dipped in shadow, but the sight of the tumbled wastepaper basket with its contents strewn at his master's feet made him shut his mouth and breathe carefully.

Although the library faced south and had three windows, it was a sombre room. The moss-green velvet hangings were never completely drawn aside, and the ruched and gathered tulle curtains, once white, were now so dusty that each fold was traced by a line of grey. The divan was draped with a Persian rug and strewn with cushions of gold and silver brocade, the covers of which could easily have been identified by old friends of the family as being discarded ball dresses of the late lamented Mrs. Marek. The black book-cases reached to the ceiling and were filled in such a manner

11

that the finely bound and gilt-edged volumes stood on the upper and middle shelves, while the paper-backed and bedraggled books occupied the lower regions, irrespective of their contents. A settee and two armchairs of red repp were grouped in a corner near the stove round a table with a blue and red brocade cover trimmed with a tarnished gold fringe, and all the other stands and shelves and small tables in the room had similar brocade covers. Even the small and fashionable objects which litter a man's room, the case for playing-cards and the brush for the card table, the appointments book and the blotter, were backed with brocade and enriched with gold braid. A lamp with a domed brown shade was suspended by brass chains from the ceiling like a sinister mushroom.

After staring silently at some papers on the desk in front of him, Richard Marek turned his head and said lightly: 'What's that you were saying?'.

Joseph opened his mouth and distended his broad nostrils with a look of relief. 'It's the books you lost, sir. I found them – downstairs.'

'Put them back where they belong. I have been looking for them everywhere. Why didn't you bring them up sooner? Do you expect me to write you a post card next time?'

Joseph emitted the short and sheepish laugh which was expected from him and then resumed his habitual impenetrable countenance, that mixture of knowing and not knowing which is acquired by military batmen of long standing.

Richard Marek shifted his position, crunched some crumpled papers beneath his feet and finally kicked them out of the way.

'You showed her out, did you?'

'I did, sir.'

'What did she want, Joseph?'

'The Baroness did not say, sir.'

'But she said something, didn't she? She was not struck dumb, was she?'

'At your service, sir. She said she would come another day and then she passed some personal remarks about the downstairs curtains.'

'Which ones?'

'The blue ones, at your service, sir.'

Richard Marek gripped the edge of the desk with both hands, bent his elbows, squared his shoulders, and in this pugnacious attitude he looked ahead of him.

'Ha,' he said. 'She did? The bitch. May she perish.' And he silently continued to stare into space with his somewhat bulging blue eyes, the same as those of his sister. He had also the same square forehead and short blunt nose, but he lacked the distinction of her long-necked, tall and portly figure; he was of broad and robust build, with the over-developed thighs and curved legs of the horseman. His hair, once red, had faded into a yellowish grey, more from the effects of an outdoor life than age, but it was still thick and wavy. His cheeks and neck were ruddy and freckled and so were his hands. For many years he had served in a crack cavalry regiment and while he did not pride himself on his horsemanship, which was for him more or less a matter of course, he claimed to be equally good at most sports and games, an all-round sportsman, in his own words, which was why many people called him behind his back the 'all-round'.

The dog's whining interrupted the stillness. 'It's the animal, sir. He is wondering if he can come in.'

'He is? Why doesn't he come in, for God's sake? The door is open. Am I to send him a post card as well? What's the matter today? First you and then Rollo. So much delicacy of feeling – I am overwhelmed. And why, I should like to know? Do I bite? Have I ever bitten you?'

Then, raising his voice: 'Here, Rollo. Here, sir.'

The spaniel appeared, treading softly, and although he held his tail low, he wagged it in a tentative way.

'And now, Joseph,' continued Richard Marek, 'now that you are here, put out my hat and my gloves. I am going to see my cousin. I had not meant to go, but now I do. I feel like a fight and he always rouses my spleen.'

'He is very pleasant when he comes here, sir.'

'Yes, I know all about it. To you he is. Hallo, Joseph, he says, and how long have you been with the family? And the next time he asks you the same again, because he never listened in the first place. That's not pleasant. That's arrogant. And when I make a feeble joke – I know it's feeble, of course – he never laughs. Do you call that pleasant? No manners. And no heart. And I don't know which is worse.'

He turned to the desk again and rummaged among his papers. The spaniel lay down at his feet and yawned.

'Come here, Joseph; I can't find my glasses. It's either this or this. I had them all sorted out. Now read this out to me. What does it say on the top?'

'Quarterly report of the shareholders, at your service, sir.'

'Good. That's the document I wanted. Now you take it and wrap it up for me. But don't roll it up like an omelette; fold it in four and keep it flat. That will give him something to get on with. To get on with, I say, because that's only the beginning. This shareholding business – it's as temperamental as a racehorse, and not as enjoyable. You own something, and then again, you don't own enough to have your say in it. Sometimes I get so tired that I think I'll put the whole caboodle of these reports and grocers' bills in the fire and go and hire myself out as a stable master to a travelling circus.'

'You would not do that, sir.'

'And why not?'

'Because it's not honourable.'

'Honourable. What's honourable? To have a duel with a fellow because he said something you did not like and which was probably quite true, and perhaps to kill the poor devil, that's honourable; and to mess about with a girl and then set the family lawyer on to her and buy her a tobacco shop because she is not Society and you haven't got the guts to face the music, that's honourable; and to run up debts with the local tradesmen because you are cavalry and must live up to your rank, for the sake of your Emperor and country, that's honourable, too.'

During this speech Richard Marek had turned away from his servant, had approached the window and had continued with a lowered voice as though he were not speaking to anyone present, but addressing a person who only existed in his mind.

The spaniel followed him and put a paw on his trouser leg. His master bent down, clasped the dog's paw and stroked his ear.

'There,' he said, 'look at this, Joseph. You said just now what I could not do, and I suppose I could not, no matter

15

how much I talk. And Rollo here sticks to me, although I lost my temper with him a while ago, because that's how he is and he can't change his spots either. And if I die, he might even starve himself to death out of grief, although it won't do anybody any good, and there will be two more fools out of the world. The only difference is, Joseph, that he does not know he is a fool and I do. That is, sometimes. And so are you.'

'At your service, sir.'

CHAPTER 3

JOSEPH SAW his master to the door after administering a perfunctory brushing down of the lapels and collar of his coat. Then, with Rollo leading the way, he went through a leather-covered and brass-studded door which opened on to the servants' quarters. A narrow passage without windows connected the kitchen and the stillroom and received its share of daylight from an open square cut out of the back door and covered with wire netting, to keep the flies out. He lifted the latch and went into the yard of the house.

It was a flagged square with a tall acacia growing in one corner. The tree was in bloom and the curly blossoms hung in long white streaks over the black bark. Within the enclosed space formed by the adjoining houses, the air was hot and still; the scent of the flowers mingled with the smell of drains.

The spaniel trotted briskly round and refreshed himself, while Joseph sniffed and wiped his nose with the back of his hand, a luxury in which he only indulged when alone. His glance wandered from the dog to the low-roofed washhouse in the background, flanked by ash cans and piles of firewood, to the three empty and derelict stables and to the tiers of slatternly balconies above them, with the cords for the beating of carpets drawn in a criss-cross pattern to and fro across the rusty iron railings, and with their perennial vegetation of ragged brooms and mops, dishcloths and broken saucepans.

He called to the dog and returned to the kitchen, where the cook sat on the bench by the cold stove, grinding coffee. 'The Major has gone out,' he informed her, well aware that she knew it already, but he felt that he owed it to his position to be in the know about everything that concerned his master.

The cook, a tall and sinister person with abundant black hair, masterful eyebrows and a fierce hooked nose, gave him a look like a conspirator, while she turned the flashing brass handle as though she were stirring a witches' brew.

'He says he may not be in for dinner. And if he is not in, in time, we are not to wait.'

'And what am I to do about the beef? It won't keep overnight. It's all very well to give orders, but they must make sense.'

'Orders always make sense. And he likes to keep fixed hours, and when he does not keep fixed hours it's because he does not want to keep them, and then he does not like to be reminded of the fact that he didn't keep them. You've got to have everything tidy and stick to rules.'

'Yes,' said the cook. 'I know about his rules. He always talks about them and every day it's a different one. And his tidiness – you make me laugh, you do.' She pierced him with another dark look. 'Not a day goes past that he cannot find his keys or his glasses, and it's a good thing he was with the Horse Guards, because a horse is all in one piece and does not fall to bits, and you can't lose it.'

'Oh, can't you?' And Joseph crossed his arms behind his back, put one foot forward and looked down at her through half-closed eyes, an attitude of elegant haughtiness which he had obviously copied from an idol of long past military glory. It was wasted on her or seemed to be.

'I'll get the coffee ready now,' she told him with ill-restrained brutality and she wrenched the small drawer with the grounds out of the mill and held it in her hands, weighing it thoughtfully. 'It's a shame,' she continued. 'Goes out all upset because she called on him and likely off his food for the day and here I am with the beef on my hands and it won't last the night out. I wonder what she wanted.'

She rose, and in the sunlight falling over her figure the grease spots on her blue apron shone like stars on the sky. A bell rang.

Joseph suddenly dropped his lordly attitude, turned quickly round, and, running a finger over his hair and neckcloth, he left the kitchen hurriedly.

In front of the door he found a stranger of about thirty-eight. He wore a light hat and a pale, elegant overcoat. A grey pearl pin was stuck in his tie. He held a pair of yellow gloves in one hand and a cane in the other.

He had been running sharp, quick glances over the carved porch above the entrance and the polished brass ring on the door; at the windows with their white-painted sashes and the carved stone garlands above them, all the things which give opulence and stateliness to the façade of a house.

By the time the servant appeared his glance had become bored and tired.

'Is this the house of Major – eh – Marek?' he asked with that hesitation in the voice which is a veiled insult.

'That is right, sir. Mr. Marek now.' And Joseph stared straight ahead of him with his hand pressed to the seam of his trousers.

'Is he in?'

'No sir, and we don't know when to expect him back.'

'Indeed,' said the man in a tired voice, but he gave the servant a quick look full in the face, as though to convince himself of the truth of the statement.

'He's used to being snubbed,' thought Joseph. 'And when he can, he snubs others himself.'

The stranger now lifted his pointed eyebrows, twisted his mouth and stuck an eyeglass in his left eye. His features were handsome, long and pointed, and the monocle suited him admirably, while the band of black-ribbed silk which was attached to it gave a certain splendour to his fair brows and lashes.

'I should have liked to see him. A – pity. I am rather busy and I don't know when – however, it cannot be helped. Here is my card. Which is the best time, do you think? Perhaps in the morning? I might be able to – manage it.'

'The master always rides out in the morning, sir. But he is back by eleven. Is there a message?'

'No. Just give him my card. And – eh – thank you.'

Joseph received it on the salver with the respectful indifference of the well-trained servant. Then he shut the door none too softly.

He replaced the salver on the stand, bent over and read aloud: 'Ferdinand Lajos Gideon, Count Szalay.'

A minute later he said to the cook: 'A Hungarian Count. Never seen him before.'

'You've seen him now. Here is your coffee.'

'A Count. And a Hungarian. He is no good.'

'Drink up. It's getting cold.'

'The Hungarians are always a pack of trouble. And when they are Counts they are something special, and then it's special trouble. They never were any good to anybody.'

She put a lump of sugar in her mouth and gulped some coffee down without a word.

'And I say they are no good. And if it wasn't for their Tokay and their pigs, they wouldn't have anything at all.'

The cook crunched the sugar. 'That's all empty talk. Either you are some good or you aren't, and it does not help matters if you are a Chinaman with a plait or a Bohemian dressed up like a monkey.' And she approached and stuck a finger into Joseph's neckcloth. 'And that about what they've got and haven't got is not true either. Because in Vienna they don't know how to fry a decent Vienna steak the way we do it in Prague, and then again in Vienna they make the real Hungarian gulash much better than in Hungary, and that's God's truth and goes to show that you can't go by names and countries. And call Rollo now. He wants his coffee the same as you do.'

CHAPTER 4

BEHIND A HIGH stone wall surmounted by iron spikes whose points stuck into the air like bayonets lay the residence of Baron Kreslov. The long stretched main front overlooked a fair-sized garden with a few symmetrical flower beds, a banked lawn and shrubs bordering the yellow gravel paths. The house had been built only fifteen years before and was a light grey stone building with a pillared veranda on the ground floor and a curved balcony with a florid iron balustrade above it. It had white shutters, green Venetian blinds and a rose-red tiled roof of Baroque design. 'Less would have been more,' said some people, and others said: 'It's not a house; it's an hotel.'

In the car, the lower part of the windows were of frosted glass, to prevent passers-by from looking inside, but the top of the panes were of clear glass, so that, as she approached her home, the Baroness could see for a while the upper story of the house, where the hot April sun struck blinding flashes of silver from the white shutters; then a square of turf and bushes, the light green turned to a yellowish grey and the dark green to black in the strong light. After that, the high, iron-spiked wall barred the view. The Baroness sat silently and still, with her gloved hands clasped over her bag in her lap. After having looked into the dazzling daylight, the dimness inside the car hurt her eyes. She longed to close her lids, but refused herself this indulgence, so that instead of seeing Anton's shoulders in the fawn livery, the straight-cut hair at the nape of his neck and the band of glossy brown leather round his cap, she saw nothing but red rings sliding into a black expanse in increasingly widening circles, like the surface of water which has been ruffled by a stone.

'It is unusually hot for the time of the year,' she thought after the affliction had passed, and remembering the blue curtains in her brother's drawing-room, a feeling of indignation took hold of her. In order to force herself to remain calm, she lifted the speaking-tube from a silver hook by her side.

'It is amazingly hot for the time of the year,' she said in a voice which was mild and commanding at the same time.

In faint and distorted sounds the answer came back: 'Indeed, it is, madam.'

'And that blue, that vulgar sky-blue,' she thought. 'Just the shade she would choose. The taste of that breed. And the grand piano which she could not play. Perfect. All it needs is a silk couch and the picture is complete.'

'Don't drive up, Anton,' she said into the tube. 'I will let myself in through the street door. Take the car straight to the garage, otherwise the paintwork will get cracked in the sun.'

'Madam thinks of everything.'

'I have to, Anton,' she replied with great dignity. 'The taste of a——' she thought. 'A dead one. But dead or alive, it does not make her any better.'

The noise of the engine stopped and she saw that they had

arrived. Already Anton stood outside, cap in hand, holding the door open. As she rose from her seat she felt a pain in her palm, and glancing down, she saw that her fingers were clenched in a strangely twisted and rigid grasp and a seam of her black glove had burst open beneath the thumb, revealing a forked blue vein on the white flesh.

'I hope you will have good news from your wife soon,' she said kindly. 'I will go and see her when she is better.'

'She will be delighted. Thank you very much, madam.'

CHAPTER 5

THERE WAS no reason to sit there, but owing to a habit formed through many years, Fräulein Lotte was sitting in the sewing-room on the first floor, by the open French window which gave on to the balcony. A warm breeze bent the purple, bell-shaped flowers which grew in boxes beneath the balustrade and moved the rings of the white muslin curtains with a cheerful rattling noise. The room was narrow and lined with white-painted cupboards and contained two sewing-machines, a little table and a few old chairs with frayed cane seats. An ironing-board stood folded up in one corner. The rooms adjoining to the right and left had once been the day and night nurseries of the Kreslov children, and in those days the sewing-room held the same strategical advantages as a hill commanding the battlefront. Several years ago, however, the rooms had been transformed and redecorated. Similarly, Fräulein Lotte had discarded her former occupation as nursery governess and had become housekeeper and confidante in general; thus she was removed from the sphere of English and French governesses and tutors, who, in bygone days, had contested her position of authority.

She was a woman of forty-five, a teacher's daughter from

Dresden. Her figure and bearing could have been the envy of any guardsman, as she stood six feet in her stocking feet, was as lean and straight as a hop pole and – unlike most inordinately tall people, who usually slouch – she kept her shoulders well back and held her head high. Winter and summer alike, she dressed in black with white starched collars, wore her straight brown hair twisted into an old-fashioned knot and allowed as her only extravagance a pair of long black jet earrings which dangled strangely at the sides of her good, faithful, snub-nosed face. In this get-up she could move between the servants' hall and the drawing-room without ever being taken for servant or master. This was a great relief to the Baroness, who had once passed through a most unpleasant experience.

During the first years of her marriage she had engaged as a housekeeper a presentable-looking woman, not too young – she was careful about this – an officer's widow with good references. At an afternoon reception this person helped, as usual, to pour out the tea and hand round the dishes. On this occasion the most distinguished guest, the doyen of the Diplomatic Corps in Prague, approached his hostess with the request 'to be presented to this charming young woman, who, I see, is an intimate friend of yours'. The Baroness went white and red and so petrified with shock that, as she said, if a flash of lightning had struck next to her, she would not have jumped.

That evening, after the guests had left, she dismissed the unfortunate widow who was guilty of having looked like a 'lady', which, after all, is equivalent to what the lawyers call false pretences. This event would have been distressing enough as it was, but it hurt the Baroness all the more as she herself felt partly responsible for bringing it about. It was her habit at the time to make the housekeeper wear the good black dresses which she herself had discarded, one of the many small economies on which she prided herself. The fact that the widow had turned traitress so to speak, in one of her own mistress's gowns, was an insult which the Baroness never forgot: 'I gave her my friendship until I found out that I had been nursing a viper in my bosom.' After this, people whispered behind her back that only the Baroness's corset-maker knew how big that friendship had been.

As soon as Fräulein Lotte heard the muffled sounds of voices and footsteps downstairs, she put aside her mending-basket and passed through a corridor which divided the whole length of the first floor and which, with its white-washed walls and grey linoleum, had that air of melancholy cleanliness peculiar to hospitals.

As she descended the stairs, she saw the Baroness standing in the hall in conversation with the young footman, while two maids were carrying away her hat, gloves and fur stole. The hall was formal and splendid with Oriental rugs, numerous large oil paintings darkened by age, whose gilt frames shimmered between the foliage and fronds of ever-green plants and palm trees which grew in embossed bronze vessels. Fräulein Lotte was used to it all and therefore it never occurred to her to reflect about the astonishing contrast between the reception rooms and the floor above. It was as though the house were leading a double life of its own which expressed the two conflicting attitudes of its mistress; on the one hand the desire to display her wealth to the outside world, and on the other hand, an urge to deprive herself of all the luxuries in the secluded part of her existence, in order to soothe her bad conscience. For, rightly or wrongly, the Baroness felt guilty because she was the wife of one of the wealthiest men in the country, and she often tried to hide the outward signs of it. This was why, for instance, she had made Anton wait with the car in a deserted side street, although it was an ordeal for her to walk the few hundred yards from her brother's house through the crowded thoroughfare of the Wenzelsplatz.

'Well, madam. Back so soon? You hardly left half an hour ago.'

'We took a short cut on our way back,' replied the Baroness. 'It is amazingly hot; I must open my jacket. I have been longing to do this all the time.' And while she unbuttoned the coat of her tailor-made suit, she gave a smile of endearing frankness, the smile of the *grande dame* who does not stand on her dignity.

'And tea, Karl, do you hear?' she continued to the footman. 'In there.' And she pointed with her chin towards one of the folding glass doors behind which lay the smallest of the drawing-rooms.

'And once you have brought it in, you need not wait. Fräulein Lotte will do the rest.'

With this she hooked her hand under Fräulein Lotte's arm and led her away.

As soon as they were alone, she sat down and passed a hand over her forehead. 'I am not angry,' she said. 'I am sad. Yes, very sad. It is queer, really, when you come to think of it, after all these years, all these years, and yet it hurts me as much as on the first day. And perhaps it is not so strange. After all, he is my brother.'

The housekeeper nodded. 'But at least, I hope, he was pleasant?'

The Baroness laughed. 'Pleasant. My dear Lotte. He was neither pleasant nor unpleasant; he was not at all, for the simple reason that I never saw him.'

'He was not in?'

'Of course he was in, very much so; he could be heard all over the place. And this Joseph, the creature, stood stock still and never did a thing. He should have gone up and announced me or at least asked for a message, but I dare say that would have been too much effort. I was shocked. But not surprised. A dog takes after his master and a household takes after its mistress, and even if she is dead, she is still there. My brother never had much say in anything and he does not care and lets things slide, and of course the servants are glad to muddle along. You can imagine in what a state the house is. The curtains upstairs are black with dirt; I could see it already from the street. Just as it always was, during her lifetime.'

'It was never well kept, as places go,' replied Fräulein Lotte. 'Of course, I have not seen it for some time, but I still recall it.'

'I am sure you do. And this carelessness about everything. Hair-raising, believe me. The curtains exposed to the sun. I spoke to Joseph about it, but I might have saved my breath. I still care too much; I can't help it. It is foolish of me, but there it is.'

'You are much too good, madam. But I am sure next time you will find Mr. Marek more like himself.'

'I should certainly hope so. When he throws a fit of temper, I can always make excuses to people and say it is his grief. But with me he cannot pretend. He was as glad as we all were when she died; I know it perfectly well and he is annoyed that I know it. That's the way he is. Instead of being grateful for my sympathy, and God knows I am the last person to withhold it, he——'

She broke off and they both looked up as a slight clattering noise outside announced the approaching tea equipage. The Baroness folded her hands on her lap with a kindly expression, while Fräulein Lotte rose and gave her directions to the footman.

'The tea here,' she said. 'And leave the plates on the trolly. And have some hot water ready in case it should be wanted.' All this gravely and thoughtfully, as though he had never served the tea before and she had never supervised it.

'No, I cannot say I am surprised,' said the Baroness after the footman had withdrawn and she received her cup.

'No, don't offer me anything; I am still too upset – perhaps later. As I was saying, wasting and spending is always typical of these – these persons. *Après nous le déluge*, that was the motto of Louis Quinze, and it was not really his, but belonged to the Pompadour who ruled him. And she was that sort of woman, too, of course. There is no sense of responsibility in such creatures and they have not got the decency to think of what follows in their wake. Of course, I don't pretend to know how their minds work, but I have seen the results.'

'You are always so right, madam,' replied the house-keeper. 'I have felt this myself, but I could never put it so well.' And while the Baroness sat still, with the steaming cup raised to her lips, Fräulein Lotte bent sideways and helped herself to two slices of bread and butter and ham with stealthy movements and with a troubled expression. For although she was hungry, she was ashamed to eat and felt that she should have remained fasting out of sympathy for her mistress. She munched and swallowed hastily while the long earrings dangled round her face. Then she took a sip of tea, wiped her mouth carefully so as not to stain the napkin and said: 'And yet, the late Mrs. Marek had only to copy you, madam – as much as was within her power, of course. When I think how careful you are about everything. When I look at this handbag, for instance – I remember it already when I first came; it was not new then. And that is eighteen years ago.'

The Baroness nodded and sighed. The long life of her bags was always a subject of great pride to her and she never forgot to mention it to the ladies of her acquaintance. Yet she always forgot to add that her bags were mounted in real gold and were fastened with clasps of real rubies or sapphires and that they were relined and refurbished by her jeweller every year.

With her wardrobe the position was more difficult. Yet it was well known to her friends that she only persuaded herself to order new dresses so as to send the old ones to charitable institutions. And indeed, this was only the smallest part of her social activities. She thought of it now and her mind dwelt on the list of subscriptions which she still had on her and which had been one of the reasons for her afternoon call. The main reason, she told herself. She put her cup down with a decisive movement. 'I shall see my brother tomorrow,' she said, looking straight ahead of her. 'I must know how much he will give. The committee is waiting for the list.' And she sat upright and lowered her chin so that a majestic fold appeared beneath it. 'Perhaps you will telephone, Lotte. Tomorrow morning – or, better still, tonight – and say that my brother can expect me tomorrow at three in the afternoon. And now I will go upstairs and look through the other lists and see what is still outstanding. Bring up the receipts and the books so that they are ready when the accountant arrives. My husband is sending him today, isn't he?'

'Yes, madam. The Baron sent a message that the man would be here by five.'

'And Miss Griffith is coming at six, isn't she? What are we going to do with her? Hedwig won't be home in time and I don't feel like having a lesson. Will you take her over, Lotte? You really like it, don't you? And read on in the novel from where we stopped last time and then tell me whom she married in the end – that is, if you get as far. And if at all. And if you feel tired, walk Miss Griffith round the garden and ask her the name of the flowers in English, and about that bit in Rudy's letter, you know. And ask her if she knows where Kensington Gardens is and if she thinks it suitable for lodgings for a young man. I think my husband will want to hear about it. And then ask her to stay for dinner – we did not ask her last time, so I think she is due.'

She rose, and so did her companion.

'And shall I have the usual parcel ready, madam?'

'Yes, by all means. And also a pot of flowers, Lotte. Cyclamens. Have a look what he can spare in the greenhouse. Miss Griffith likes flowers and I felt so awkward when Franz made that remark the other day about the English being such a Christian nation – every time they say

Christ they mean cotton. It was said as a joke, of course, but I don't think she liked it.'

'The Baron has a sense of humour all his own, madam.'

'Quite. He thinks he is funny.'

'We all have our foibles, madam.'

'Yes, Lotte. Everybody has them, and with most people it does not matter, but when one is in my husband's position one simply cannot afford it. You know what the world is like, and one little remark goes astray and all the thousands he gives away to good works are forgotten.'

'The wasps always pick the choicest fruit, madam.'

The Baroness smiled ruefully, clasped her hands to her heart and raised her eyes to the ceiling.

Fräulein Lotte straightened a chair and a cushion and thought: 'She is off again, playing to the full drawing-room, and then she will see that she is alone with me and get cross. And the Baron, he is quite right when he speaks his mind; at least he knows what he is, even if he was christened by the Archbishop of Prague.'

CHAPTER 6

It was after five o'clock in the afternoon when Richard Marek was shown into Steffanie Smejkal's drawing-room. He found her standing with her back turned to the door and contemplating a large gilded basket filled with a mass of tall-stemmed yellow roses. She plucked with one hand at the yellow satin ribbon which was twisted round the gilded handle and dangled a pair of scissors in the other.

Once a Court beauty and still very much admired, she had preserved the brittle charm of her tall and frail figure, with the small head, the graceful neck and the sloping shoulders. But already her blonde hair had lost its freshness, the skin beneath her large brown eyes was dark and tired and the yellow tinge of her throat contrasted with the pink and white of her face. She was forty-eight years old.

'Well, Steffie? This looks like a new conquest to me.'

'Not at all, Richard. An old one rediscovered. And those are the fatal ones.'

'How old?'

'Very old. In the days gone past we used to play together. As children, of course.'

'Of course.'

'And seeing these roses, it breaks my heart.'

34

'In that case, I had better sit down,' said Richard Marek.

'Stories of first love are always long because they are complicated and they are complicated because love was thwarted. And thwarted it always is, of course, because if all had gone well, the tale would not be worth telling.'

Steffanie Smejkal dropped the scissors on the floor and sat down on a stool which was placed next to the tall and narrow *trumeau*; in the old glass, flanked by two fluted pillars of walnut wood and crested with bronze laurel branches, a part of the room was reflected with a faded and greenish tinge.

'When I said that it breaks my heart, I did not mean it in this way. I only thought that it was such a waste on his part to send me two hundred yellow roses – yes, two hundred, I counted them – because I would have preferred to be given the money instead.'

'Ah, this is more like you, Steffie.'

'And apart from this, Richard, they look so ugly. They are stuck into a bed of moss, and they don't grow out of it, they bristle. Like a golden hedgehog with bristles of roses. It is not pretty, is it?'

'Perhaps not, Steffie, but the poor man, or the florist, thought they were beautifully arranged. And talking about hedgehogs, you know there is a sixteenth-century Bohemian proverb saying: "The hedgehog thinks he has got curls." So if you can imagine your conquest as a hedgehog – a dreaming hedgehog, with fancies, that goes without saying – you will perhaps feel more kindly towards him.'

'You are wrong there, Richard. That is not at all necessary. I feel kindly towards him already, and this is the worst one can feel towards a man. If a person is not very attractive and not very entertaining, you say: "Poor So-and-so, he is a

35

very decent fellow really; I wish him well." And he bores you so much that you cannot even find the energy to indulge in a bit of malicious gossip about him.'

'Well, what am I to think, Steffie? Now he bores you and he is decent and a minute ago he was an old flame and those are the fatal ones.'

'I talk a lot, when the day is long, Richard. You should know this by now. But he annoys me. Why does he have to be so correct? Why couldn't he buy me a pair of gloves instead? And last year when I met him in Karlsbad we took a promenade through the woods, and as we got to the last house, he took his hat off and on our way back he put his hat on again on exactly the same spot. That's the sort of man he is. And now, Richard, please ring for Katy and we'll have tea.'

The maid appeared, a young, blonde and smiling person, who wore her frilled cap with an air and whose prettiness would have given grave anxiety to many ladies. Steffanie, however, was not among them. And if years as a Society beauty had yellowed her skin and dug hollows round her eyes, they had also given her a composure and a facility of speech which made her more charming than ever.

The tea was placed on a cloth of old lace and poured into Dresden cups from which the gilt was almost worn off.

'But what does he look like?' asked Richard Marek and helped himself to bread and butter and cherry jam.

Steffanie Smejkal put her cup down and made a vague gesture. 'He looks like a man,' she said. 'And because he looks like one, he thinks he is one.'

The maid on her way to the door, giggled. Richard Marek waited until she had left the room.

'Really, Steffie,' he said. 'Always the same. Always playing up to the gallery and trying to get a laugh *coûte que coûte*. And if it is not the Prince, then it is the maid.'

She did not reply, but went on eating bread and jam with a robust enjoyment which went strangely with the frailty of her appearance.

'Give me more tea, Richard,' she said. 'But pour the milk first and the tea afterwards. And now tell me why you were angry today.'

'How do you know I was?'

'Because if I had made my last remark at another time you would have smiled, but today you took it up and found fault with it and were going to give me a lecture, and you would, if I did let you ramble on. And when you moralize and sermonize with other people, you only do it because you are angry with yourself, and you are angry with yourself when you meet with a situation and cannot master it. What was it?'

'Nothing, really.' And he handed her the filled cup. 'My sister called. It is exactly three years ago today that they carried Sophy out, and my God, if Melanie does not poke her nose into the house just today. She never set foot, as you know, during Sophy's lifetime, but now, I dare say, she counted it up on her fingers and thought it was a decent interval of mourning or what have you, and there she was. Why in the name of the ten baronial timber mills can't she ask me to come over to Bubenc? I go there from time to time, as you know. But having the effrontery to come to my own house, just to make it clear that now that Sophy is dead the place is fit again for the Baroness Kreslov. The nastiness of it. She must have been waiting for this day and

37

licked her chops in anticipation, like Rollo does when the cook calls him.'

'And what did she have to say, Richard?'

'Say? She said nothing. I saw to that. As soon as I heard her voice downstairs, I threw a fit of temper. I can always do it if I want to, and there's nothing like having a temper, Steffie. I learnt it in the army. A temper is like a thunder-storm, you see, an act of God, as it were, and people have to take shelter or run away and wait until it is over. Because while you have it they can't get at you.'

'And now you are ashamed of yourself.'

'If you wish it.'

'That means you aren't. But, Richard, what if the date of Melanie's call was a coincidence and she wanted something quite different, something real? Wouldn't you then be ashamed of yourself?'

'Can't say.'

'Pass me the cakes, Richard.' And Steffanie Smejkal took a couple of vanilla-scented biscuits and crunched them. 'I think you are doing her wrong, you know. She called on me yesterday. For the Silesian Holiday Camp charity.'

'Oh.'

'And probably that was the reason why she came to see you today.'

'Not on your life. For this she would have sent round her German female grenadier.'

'I am not so sure,' replied Steffanie Smejkal. 'You are not fair to her. She is very fond of you, *au fond*. And very broad-minded, I think.'

'Of course she is. When it suits her. She is too clever to be narrow. Isn't this a new vase you have got over there?'

He pointed to a white china swan which contained in its hollowed body a bunch of anemones.

'No, it is not.'

'Looks nice, though.'

Steffanie took a cigarette from a blue enamel case and twisted it between her fingers.

'The way you talk, Richard. Is this new and then you tell me that the flowers look pretty. Of course they do, because I put them there. And with this you think you've got away and need not answer. You are too hard on Melanie, my dear man. And now give me a light.'

'It's no good, Steffie. I cannot forgive her. It was her horrible broadmindedness about Sophy which egged me on. And if she had not been so monstrously understanding about men's affairs – and she has no idea about them – and offered to pay up for me and settle her, out of her own money on top of it——'

'Which was handsome of her, Richard.'

'So it was. And smug and self-satisfied into the bargain. How I hate these good women. They'll do anything for you, but in such a way as to make it all wrong.'

'But this is not really what you hold against her, Richard.'

'I suppose it is not. The worst came after. That is to say, I was a fool. And Melanie was right. But enough of it. If one is ugly one does not stand in front of the mirror, and if one is stupid one does not like to dwell on it.'

For a while they continued silent, while Steffanie smoked with her head thrown back and with a pretty display of her long white hands.

Richard Marek stroked his head and stared at the top of his shoes.

'All right,' he said at last. 'I'll see what she wants tomorrow, and I will try——'

They were interrupted by the entrance of Mr. Smejkal, followed by another man who, by the way he stopped at the door and by his forced and stiff attitude, made it obvious that he was a newcomer in the house and was waiting for his host to give him a lead.

Mr. Smejkal was a stout man in his fifties, with a glistening pink bald head encircled by a fair fringe of hair. He had watery blue and bloodshot eyes whose look inspired confidence, and dimples in his cheeks when he smiled, which he nearly always did. He was dressed carefully, with touches of old-fashioned elegance, the high wing collar, the unusually large and solemn tie and the dove-coloured spats.

After he had kissed his wife's hand, he turned to Richard Marek.

'I suppose I came home too early,' he said. 'Still, here I am. Everybody has a place in this world, even husbands, eh, Marek?'

'You said it. Not I.'

'So I did. Keep me in my place and crush me. Steffie, I appeal to you.'

'Leave poor Richard in peace, Poldi.'

'Shall be done, if you say so. That's the sort of man I am. Always obliging, Marek. And where does it get me, I ask you? Still, never mind. I will unburden myself another time. As you see, I have brought up a reinforcement. Steffanie, I present to you Mr. Maly, who has come all the way from Pardubice, from the shores of the Elbe.'

Steffanie Smejkal extended her hand and made the visitor sit down on the settee beside her. He was of about the same age as her husband, a tall and important-looking man, with a round face, thinning dark hair, round eyes behind round glasses and a small mouth which made him look like a serious owl. His sombre clothes, together with his grave bearing, made her think of a don at a provincial university.

'What a charming room this is, dear madam,' he remarked. 'It is so seldom that one——. But this is real taste. And besides, it is made for a delightful spring day like this. The sun on the green and yellow striped walls, for instance. Mr. Marek, please look. It is well worth seeing.'

'I know. Like spinach and egg.'

Mr. Smejkal threw himself into a chair and gurgled with laughter, while his wife smiled charmingly and Richard Marek stroked his hair, wrinkled his nose and looked dubious.

Mr. Smejkal recovered from his fit of hilarity and said: 'Maly, you old scoundrel, talking of fresh young green, and the only green you know is the cover of the board-room table and perhaps the billiard cloth. And now, gentlemen, what can I do for you? Whisky and Seltzer or one of those frenchified apéritifs or a peach brandy or a cherry brandy? Bools or Heering. We've got it; it's all here for the asking.'

Mr. Maly turned slowly and gave a delightful smile all round. He had such small, white and even teeth, and his expression was so angelic, that everyone was surprised.

'Whisky, please,' he said and continued to look cherubic.

It turned out that everybody wanted whisky, except Steffanie, who decided on a peach brandy.

'Marek, you have an expensive family,' began Mr. Smejkal. 'The Baroness called yesterday – I daren't call her Melanie, not even behind her back, you know – and when she left, we were five hundred crowns poorer.'

'But I gave your sister some very good advice, Richard,' broke in Steffanie Smejkal.

'Ah, your sister is a Baroness, Mr. Marek?' asked Mr. Maly. 'But you, you are not——'

'No, I am not.'

'What is the name, may I ask?'

'Kreslov, if that's any good to you.'

'Ah, yes.' He pondered, not seeing or perhaps not wanting to see how the others exchanged looks with raised eyebrows. 'Is there a connection – forgive my questions, I am not asking out of curiosity, but it interests me – is there a tie with the sawmills and timber?'

'Certainly. Now, Steffanie, please, your advice. I am all ears.'

'Quite simple, Richard. I told her that in future, when she starts on her begging tour, she should send a pretty young girl instead. Especially for making the rounds of the banks and business houses. And would you believe it, she was most enthusiastic. She saw it at once. I told you she was broadminded.'

'What a profound knowledge of human nature you have, dear madam,' remarked Mr. Maly. 'Of course, I am not surprised. As soon as I saw you I knew you were a woman of the world.'

Mr. Smejkal looked at him for a second with an unpleasant and questioning eye. Then he laughed.

Richard Marek flushed slightly and rose with a look of disgust.

'I kiss your hand, Steffie,' he said. 'And, Smejkal, my compliments to your whisky. Mr. Maly, it was entertaining and perhaps we shall see each other again. Are you leaving, too? If it is agreeable, I will accompany you. This part of the town can be rather confusing if one is not familiar with it. Especially after – what did you say it was? Domazlice?'

'No. Pardubice.'

'Ah, yes.' And with this he took hold of the other's arm. After the visitors had left, Steffanie Smejkal threw herself on the settee.

'Really, Poldi,' she said. 'Was this necessary?'

'It was. You won't believe it, but he is a very shrewd business man. And his smile helps. Others have to bargain. He just sits and shows his teeth. That is sufficient.'

'The things he said, Poldi.'

'Come, Steffanie, that's understandable. When he comes into a drawing-room he loses his head and behaves as he was taught forty years ago. Just keep talking, that's all that matters. That's what used to be called conversation.'

'And he called me a woman of the world. I suppose a little bird whispered something in his ear. He says it and thinks it is flattering, but in reality it is a double-edged compliment. When someone wants to bring up a *risqué* story or tell something which would not be possible in a decent house, then it is always: "But you will understand; you are a woman of the world." How I hate it! And then again, it means that I am at least thirty-five. A woman of the world is never less.'

CHAPTER 7

WHEN THE two men stepped into the street, the sun had already disappeared, and now the April sky was marbled pink and blue, dipped into a melting light of an exhausted and yet brooding sweetness, a glow of autumnal overripeness which had nothing to do with the time of the year. On their right lay Kampa Island. Already the foliage drooped from the dusty trees, already the blades of the ragged lawn showed yellow tips. The smell of the young and tired green mingled with the breath of decomposition which came up from the river.

The Moldau rose and sank in sluggish waves beneath the Karl's Bridge, yet it did not seem to move. Thus it looked as though it were the same stale mass of water which reflected for ever the old and used arches and the grey saints' figures bent above them.

'Wonderful part of the town, this Kleinseite,' remarked Mr. Maly. 'But a bit uphill and far away. I am staying at the Hotel Sroubek. Excuse me, but are you near there as well?'

'A bit farther on. Above the Museum.'

'That must be very nice. Very convenient. And your sister, the Baroness, she lives there, too?'

'No. In quite a different district.'

'Not in the Kleinseite, by any chance?'

'No.'

They passed beneath the vault of the bridge towers and on to the bridge. There were few people about, looking small and slightly ludicrous as they hastened past the crumbling nobility of the statues. Red trams clanged their way alongside the quay, their bells ringing with a feeble and ineffective tinkle. And while ahead of them the river was starred with the light of the street lamps, it sank behind their backs into the darkness of the falling night.

'You see, I am asking because I feel so out of touch nowadays,' continued Mr. Maly and gave his companion one of his smiles which startled by their unexpected radiance.

'Since the war, I am told, all the old palaces of the nobility on the Kleinseite have been turned into foreign embassies. Is that correct? And nobody lives there any more. I mean, what one calls nobody. And after this, you can picture my astonishment when Mr. Smejkal takes me to his flat and it is in the Kleinseite. Of course, the view is beautiful.'

'Quite so,' replied Richard Marek and offered his companion a cigarette. 'And so you are comfortable at the Sroubek?'

'I don't know yet. I only arrived this morning. Before the war I used to stay at the White Star. The food was very good, but there were bugs. Not in all the rooms, of course, only in certain ones. But as I said, excuse me, but don't you think it is rather eccentric of the Smejkals to live in the Kleinseite? It is so shut off from the centre of the town. And she is such a pretty woman – I dare say she prefers to keep quiet – *procul discordibus armis* – he is her second husband,

45

isn't he? I could not ask him outright, but I heard something to that effect.'

'In that case, you were told wrong,' replied Richard Marek. 'He is Steffanie's first husband. Now perhaps you would like to stop and have a last look at the castle on the hill, before we lose the view from our sight?'

They had arrived at the old town mill, where beneath the turreted tower of patched brickwork the water pours in foam-crested jets, shrieking and sibilant, between the slanting structure of wooden beams.

They halted and turned round.

'Wonderful!' exclaimed Mr. Maly. 'This is unique in the whole world. There is nothing like it, not even in Vienna. And he is her first husband, you say. You see, I am asking all these questions because you seem to know them very well. And I like to sort things out properly, don't you? There is nothing worse than irresponsible gossip. Besides, with me, you need not worry. I am like the grave.'

They continued their walk, Richard Marek smoking silently and looking neither right nor left, while the other talked, accompanying his words with comfortable and expansive gestures. 'When I said second husband, I expressed myself rather tactfully, you understand? I meant to say that Smejkal is her second, because the first one was so exalted in rank that he could not be her husband at all, do you see? He was an Archduke, wasn't he? And she was a lady-in-waiting, I am told. As soon as I saw her, I said to myself, "What a beauty." I quite understand the Archduke. I could almost lose my head myself, if I were not careful. I know you won't believe me when you see me like this, but I can be

46

rather dangerous to women. I cannot explain it myself.
Now, who was he, do you know? I suppose you knew her
already in Vienna?'

'Mrs. Smejkal was never in Vienna at all. That is, she
never lived there,' said Richard Marek. 'She was attached for
years to the house of Prince Muellweck-Hohenlingen, of the
Hohenlingen-Lippe-Detmold branch. And it was not a
Court, properly speaking, because at that time he was not a
reigning Prince any more, and——'

'Ah, so it was a Prince?'

'And as it was not a proper Court, she could not be lady-
in-waiting, naturally. *Ça va sans dire.* She was companion to
the Princess, that's all.'

'Ah, I see. There was a Princess. And tell me, she did not
mind?'

'Who did not mind what?'

'The Princess did not mind Mrs. Smejkal and Mrs.
Smejkal did not mind the Princess?'

'I am afraid I have not explained myself very well to you,'
replied Richard Marek in a stony voice. 'As I told you, Mrs.
Smejkal acted as a lady companion to the Princess. They
were very fond of each other.'

'That probably made it still worse,' replied Mr. Maly
blissfully. 'Of course, the aristocracy is very broadminded.
I could tell you stories – such stories. Excuse me – and the
Prince, he is still alive?'

'No. He died years ago. But I can assure you that you have
completely misunderstood the whole situation. There was
nothing in it, except what I have told you.'

'And as soon as the Prince dies, she marries Mr. Smejkal?
Or did that happen later?'

'I really don't know,' said Richard Marek, who knew very well. 'I don't see why it matters.'

'Ah, ah,' and Mr. Maly threw his cigarette away with a grand gesture and wagged his finger in his companion's face. 'I am sure you know. Only, you are bashful. But you need not be with me, you know. I am as silent as the grave. And personally, I don't mind at all. A woman like that is so much more interesting; so, you see, you can be perfectly frank with me.'

'There is nothing to be frank about, Mr. Maly, because there is nothing to hide. And here we are by the Gunpowder Tower. Now, I am afraid it is already later than I thought and so, if you will excuse me, I will jump on a tram. If you walk straight along the Graben, you will get to the square, and Sroubek is on your left-hand side.'

So saying, he walked with the other through the arcade of the tower, swung to the right and into the beginning of the Graben. There, by Leubert's delicatessen shop, they halted, in front of the windows lit by a cool and milky light which streamed from concealed electric bulbs. The perishable foodstuffs had been removed for the night, but a skilful hand had arranged a still life which hinted at more than it revealed, with raffia-covered bottles, white earthenware jars with fat black lettering and red lacquered seals and a wooden tea chest of toy proportions, the prised-off lid propped against its side. The little chest was heaped with sugared apricots, while a handful of the fruit lay tumbled on green paper vine leaves.

Mr. Maly contemplated it with his head held aslant.

'Discreet,' he said. 'Uniquely discreet. They don't go in for vulgarities, like others do, such as a hog's head with a lemon. There is nothing like Leubert's anywhere else in the world. Not even in Vienna.'

Richard Marek took his hat off and bowed faintly. But he was not to escape so soon. He found both his hands warmly clasped and was almost pulled off his feet into the other's arms. Mr. Maly thanked him profusely and repeatedly for having given him the pleasure of his company. It was all so friendly, so sincerely overflowing, so naïvely unreserved, that Richard Marek felt ashamed of his own supercilious and frigid attitude.

'And yet, the fellow is an earwig,' he said to himself. 'He crawls right inside you and never thinks that you may not relish it as much as he does.'

CHAPTER 8

THE FOLLOWING morning brought a thin rain mingled
with half-melted snow, and after it had passed a brisk wind
swept the streets dry and chased clouds across the sun, so
that a restless pattern of light and shade slipped over pavement and rooftops.

Rollo returned from his morning's outing with the fur
standing in damp wisps round his body.

'I don't like it, when it's playing cat and mouse like this,'
remarked the cook with a threatening glance at the sky, and
fetched the three pots of chives from the yard, where she
had placed them to be refreshed by the rain.

'Come on, burn up,' she said to the stove and wrenched
the iron door open with a great deal of clatter; a cloud of
soot and smoke billowed forth and she waved her hand to
disperse it, which caused Joseph to retreat to a far corner of
the kitchen, with one riding-boot in one hand and a brush
in the other.

'You'd better put your gloves on and be ready when the
Count comes, and mind you come and tell me quick if he
stays for lunch or not.'

'He will stay all right,' answered Joseph. 'And when he
leaves, he won't give a tip either. I've seen his sort before.'

She ignored him and glowered, as another black cloud issued from the range.

'I'll show you,' she said, dipped her hand into the salt jar and threw a fistful of salt into the fire with that fine recklessness peculiar to all good cooks, which makes them untidy on one hand and generous on the other.

Then, slightly soothed by the sight of the leaping, yellow flame, she shut the door and gave a quick and imperious stir to every pot and saucepan which simmered on the stove, as though to prove that, although she could not control the weather, she was still queen in her kitchen.

Rollo, sensing that her bad temper was over, jumped on to the bench by her side and sniffed the spicy air with cautiously twitching nostrils.

The bell rang.

Joseph dropped his brush. 'Keep the dog here,' he said. 'He looks a sight, not fit to be a gentleman's dog. When I am back, I'll tidy him up.' He snatched a pair of white cotton gloves from the window-sill and shuffled out in his felt shoes.

Rollo looked after him for a while, then lay down and returned his attention to the stove.

'That's right,' said the cook. 'You stay here and stay warm. Gallivanting about gets you nothing but rheumatics, and you got bones the same as everybody else.'

Richard Marek came out of his bedroom and ran down the stairs. He was still in his sports-shirt and riding-breeches, but his feet were clod in red slippers which were slightly too large and made a flopping noise at each step he took.

'My dear Count,' he cried, 'this is one of the most pleasant things that has happened to me for a long time. This is almost like what it says in the Bible – and their children and children's children – although not in that meaning, Heaven forbid. And you still are fair, I see; in those days you were so blonde, you looked almost white, but then, so many children are and grow quite dark afterwards and it does not mean a thing. And believe me, if you had come to me black-haired or with no hair at all – I would still be equally pleased to see you. I still can't believe it. After all these years.'

The Count meanwhile had shed his hat, gloves and cane and had slipped out of his coat with such a disregard for Joseph that the servant nearly dropped it.

The Count stood with the finger-tips of one hand resting on the marble table and displayed a cuff which was so brilliantly and at the same time so softly white, as only the costliest shirt silk and the most careful laundering could produce.

'The pleasure is entirely mine, Major,' he said with great affability and he bowed slightly and faintly clicked his heels together.

'Well, well, it's very good of you to say so, Count Szalay. Although I suppose you can hardly remember me, but still, you must have done so or you would not be here now, and it is very flattering, believe me. I was only a young subaltern then, and now I am an old nothing at all. Major! Ha! That's all past and gone; the old glory is gone, although glory – I am not so sure when I come to think of it now, and it was nothing much to be proud of. The Army is a sheepish sort of career, I suppose, but we were a decent crowd and tried to live up to the level of our horses. Because the horse is a noble animal and has a good influence on everything and everybody, and that's why you can always tell the cavalry from the rest.'

With this he took the Count's arm and led him into the drawing-room.

Joseph meanwhile had taken the visitor's coat, turned it over and placed it on one of the Venetian chairs in such a manner that a small tear in the lining was exposed to the view. After having thus vented his spleen, he followed his master into the room and stopped by the door.

'You can go, Joseph,' said Richard Marek. 'I will look after the Count myself, if you bring the glasses.'

'I still cannot get over it,' he continued and drew his guest on to a settee.

'Let me have a good look at you – yes – I can see your father; he had the same eyes.' And he looked for a while into the other's face with an expression of great fondness, while the corners of his eyes grew moist. Then he turned away and blew his nose.

The Count looked at him with a smile which was curiously inward, as though smiling to himself, and raised one pointed eyebrow higher than the other.

'Now, my dear Count, may I call you Ferdinand? I see you have got so many names. Lajos I leave to your fellow countrymen, and Gideon, well, that's for special occasions, that's like tails and white tie. But Ferdinand, well, that's something, that's good old Austrian and there we meet on common ground and you call me Richard. That's what your father used to call me. And here comes Joseph and we will have a drink on it.'

'You are too kind, it means a lot to me, I can assure you,

believe me,' replied the Count and continued to smile, as it were, to himself.

'This is Chateau Yquem, Ferdinand, eighteen hundred ninety six, not what I drink every day, and it is worthy of the occasion. My only regret is that your father is not with us and cannot taste it, because it would be a wine after his own heart. Still, we can't have it all. Here's to the memory of your father.'

They clinked glasses and sipped the yellow, oily wine. Richard Marek stared silently ahead of him with the fixed, unseeing stare of people who dwell on moving thoughts, while the Count leaned lightly back, his glass held with ease and elegance and let his eyes wander round the room: the sky-blue curtains looped back with silken tasselled cords, the white walls divided into oblong panels with slender strips of gilt, the pink and blue Sèvres vases on the piano, the music cabinet with its painted frieze of cymbals and flutes and the stiff legged chairs and settees which enclosed in their white and gold frames tapestries with flower garlands and bird cages.

Then his eyes returned to his host and rested thoughtfully on his blunt, redskinned and freckled face.

'So you know about my father,' he said at last after a slight hesitation.

'Yes, I heard by chance,' replied Richard Marek. 'I was not in Hungary at the time, we were garrisoned in a horrible hole of holes in Poland. Then somebody arrived with connections from Siebenbuergen, that's how I heard. It seemed very hard on you all, especially under the circumstances. A handful of children like that – you were, let me see. I was twenty when I stayed with you and then you were ten. Your father died two years later. Isn't that right?'

'Two and a half years. I was nearly thirteen at the time.'

'That's it. As I was saying, all young children and suddenly the father is dead. And your mother, poor soul. Is she still alive?'

'She is,' replied the Count and took a cigarette case from his breast pocket.

'Come, come, have one of mine, Ferdinand.'

'No, I want you to have one of these,' insisted the Count. 'They are something special. Hansi Sporek gave them to me, he is now attached to the Yugoslav Embassy.'

'Really? Is that the son of Colonel von Sporek?'

'No. His nephew.'

'Interesting. At the Yugoslav Embassy, you say? Is that where he managed to squeeze in? And here? I never knew. Hem. Yugoslavia. That's one of the new glories of the Creator. Seems that Yugoslavia is some good to somebody at last.'

'Not here. He is with them in Budapest,' replied the Count and bent forward with his lighter.

'Ha! In Budapest. And if it was not in Budapest, it could be in Prague, for that matter. And if not in Prague, then in Vienna. The more the merrier. Three separate states and three capitals, it's absolutely crazy, if you want my opinion. In the old days, it was Vienna and Vienna only. Big enough to hold them all. The cigarette is very good, though, I must admit. But that does not make it any better. It is crazy, I say, the way it is now, with every tin-pot nation sitting proudly on their own tin-pot republic. Still, let's talk about something else and more pleasant. Times change and we change with them, that's what we learnt at school and so did you, I daresay – you were with the priests in Vienna, weren't you?'

The Count nodded. 'At the Jesuit College.'

'That's it. The Theresianum. And we change with them. That's all nonsense. We don't change, that's just the trouble. If we did, I would not be sitting here now, making die-hard speeches.'

He refilled the glasses. 'Still, that's no reason why we should not enjoy the wine.'

'So your mother is still alive,' he continued after a short pause. 'Strange. Does she still live at home?'

'No. It was not possible to keep her with us. She got much worse.'

'Dreadful! Do you ever see her?'

'Very rarely. You see, she does not recognise anybody any more.'

'Dreadful!' repeated Richard Marek.

'Besides, now it would be out of the question in any case.' added the Count and traced with his finger on the table. 'There is nothing of home left. The land reform act, you know. And the rest sold up. That is to say, not sold up, but the creditors just came and took over.'

And he raised his head and smiled quietly at his host, while one pointed eyebrow stood higher than the other in his long and handsome face.

'And my brothers are all dead,' he continued. 'I suppose, you heard. They all fell in the war. All in the first three months.'

'I heard of two,' replied Richard Marek. 'And your sister?'

'She lives in America, in San Francisco,' said the Count. 'She is married, you know.' His voice grew suddenly tired.

'I never met him – I don't want to either. I am not a snob, but—— You understand.'

'I understand right enough. Dreadful! I am quite shaken. A lovely, big, flourishing family – yes, flourishing. That's the right word for it. All of you except your mother, poor soul. I still see it so well, as though it was yesterday. There was sun everywhere. Sun on the lake. Sun on the house. And the wine cellar. And your father's cellar master. And everything. And the apricots. And then nothing. Nothing at all.'

The Count looked at him from the side and put one hand on his arm.

'Do you still educate the horses?' he asked shyly.

'Ha! You remember that? Have some more, Ferdinand?' And he drained his glass.

'That's right,' he added. 'Educate them. That's how I called it. I could never stand it when people talk of breaking in a horse.'

'I know,' said the Count. 'You used to get quite angry.'

'And wasn't I right, Ferdinand? It is such a harsh and cruel word.'

There was a knock at the door.

'Come in, Joseph. I suppose you want to know what's happening on our front. But you tell me your news first, from your headquarters. Well?'

'Bouillon with egg and paprika chicken with noodles, at your service, sir.'

'Well, how does this sound to you, Ferdinand? Shall we be brave and risk it?'

'I had no intention of——'

'Nonsense. Here you are and here you stay. Don't make

57

sheeps' eyes, Joseph. That was all before your time. I had Vasek, then, the painter-batman.'

'He was small and dark and got kicked by a horse?' asked the Count quickly. 'A dappled grey, wasn't it?'

'That's right. How you remember it! My word, it warms my heart. Your father adored Vasek. He had been a house-painter before I got him and one day your father showed him a picture of the Mona Lisa and said: "Vasek, could you paint this?" And Vasek said: "Why not, sir, if I had the stencil." Haha! That's what he said: "If I had the stencil." We shall be ready in a minute, Joseph, as soon as I have changed my clothes.'

'At your service, sir.'

CHAPTER 9

It was nearly three o'clock in the afternoon when the Baroness Kreslov arrived at her brother's house and while Joseph went upstairs to announce her arrival, she put her gloves on the hall table and looped back the veil on her hat with the decisive movements of a woman who intends her visit to be a long one.

Richard Marek was sitting in his room in a chair by the window with the *Prager Tagblatt* in his hands. He was reading and making wry faces, partly because he disagreed with the text and partly because the smoke of his cigar was in his eyes. As soon as he saw Joseph, he slapped the paper down on the desk and rose, cigar in hand.

'All right, I know, I know. I am coming. Don't fuss me. I have got to die but I don't like being rushed into it. I'll take her up here, I think it's better. And then you come in and ask if you can serve the tea and then you come in again and ask if you can take it away. Make it a bit lively, eh, Joseph?' Then, already at the door, he pointed to Rollo who looked expectant and wagged his tail: 'And now, I ask you for the hundredth time: why doesn't the animal ever bark?'

He would have continued asking all sorts of pointless questions in a childish attempt to postpone the meeting, if

Joseph had not opened the door for him with a grave countenance. Richard Marek shrugged and descended the stairs while the spaniel, torn between his curiosity and the desire to stay with his master, kept on rushing down a step or two and then rushing back again, till it made one giddy to look at him.

'Ricky,' said the Baroness with a sad and melting voice.

'This is an honour indeed,' said her brother, stroking his hair and looking dubious.

'You don't mind my cigar, do you?' he added quickly. 'You are used to sorrow at home in that direction, as far as I know.'

'Franz enjoys his cigar now and then,' replied the Baroness with a pained expression.

'Exactly. That's what I meant. As I was saying, this is an honour. An unexpected honour. Out of the blue, I should say, but then, where is the blue, I ask you? If it does not rain it snows, and if it does not snow it hails – and that's April, so we are told. Not that I am surprised – nothing has been the same ever since the war – and in the old days the spring lived up to our expectations. Always nice and sunny. Isn't that so, Joseph?'

'At your service, sir.'

'There you are, Melanie. Of course, I would not dare to ask you to remember too much of the old Austrian weather. Ladies don't like to show the length of their memory. Ha!'

The Baroness clasped her hands over her bosom and looked towards the ceiling in mute indignation.

'Well, Melanie, if it's agreeable, perhaps we will go upstairs. No good standing about in the draught, is it? Once you are past twenty, you catch rheumatism, you don't know how. Still, you look very hale and hearty, I must say. Glad to see you so well, of course. But then, you cannot always go by looks unfortunately. Today red – tomorrow dead, as the proverb has it.'

Saying this, he led the way while his sister followed slightly behind him, shaking her head silently and casting short, martyred glances at his back, as though to convince an invisible audience that she was being dragged upstairs against her will and better judgment.

'Make yourself comfortable, Melanie.'

She advanced a few steps into the room and sweeping her hand in the direction of the desk with its stained and scratched leather top supported by winged and crouching sphinxes with golden hair and feet, she said: 'Ah, how nice to see it again. How it brings back old times to me.'

She turned round and stretched out her arm towards the clumsy group of red repp chairs in the corner: 'And the dear old easy chairs. I had quite forgotten you still had them. I can still see the parents. Father on the right over there and mother on the settee.'

Richard Marek drew at his cigar and listened with growing irritation, quite well aware that her words were calculated to soften him for the real purpose of her visit.

'And the other things. The carpet. Wasn't it in the smoking-room before? How well it fits in with the rest.' All this delivered in the artificially bright voice which she used when visiting orphanages.

'Goodness, and so many cushions,' she continued, bending over the divan. 'What a lot of work in them,' she added cheerfully, determined to find a good word to say about every object in the room.

'I shan't contradict you, Melanie. If you say so, it is so. I daresay you will be counting the window panes in a moment.' She sat down with her legs planted sedately in front of her, smoothed her skirt and adjusted the diamond hoop on her blouse. Their eyes, the same somewhat bulging blue eyes, met; hers powerful, his embarrassed.

'How hard you are, Ricky. Always flippant. Always your heartless little jokes. I know you don't really mean to hurt. But even so, I wish you were less – less difficult.'

'You are a goose, Melanie. Still, as you are here, I might just as well be less difficult, as you call it. Let's have it and get it over with.'

She opened her bag and unfolded a bluish green sheet of paper covered with typescript and a few signatures.

Rollo got up and sniffed it carefully.

'Aha, the Silesian holiday camp,' said Richard Marek and leaned forward with his hands on his thighs and blew curls of smoke into the air.

'A fine charity, a fine holiday for the poor children, getting them up at six every morning and making them wash. And I don't care what anybody says, no child likes to wash, rich or poor, it makes no difference.'

The Baroness pressed the sheet to her bosom and cast resigned glances at the ceiling.

'You can sing a song about it yourself, Melanie. A few drops of water down your back and: "I washed, Mademoiselle". And poor Mademoiselle with her nose in a novel, just reaching out with one hand and feeling if you are dry or wet. Why, you could have given lessons to our Seven-Dragons, how to get by.'

'You are making it up, Richard.'

'Be human just for once, Melanie. Ah, well, I suppose that would be asking too much. Never mind, hand it over. I am signing for three hundred crowns.'

'Is that the best you can do?'

'It is the same as I gave last year and I don't feel any more charitable now than I felt then. Besides, the shares are very temperamental again. You ask Franz. He will bear me out.'

'Very well, Ricky. Thank you for the three hundred. And if you really feel the pinch, why don't you have a talk with Franz? He wanted to invest some of my own money for me some months ago and I could not quite make up my mind how to arrange it. If you like, I will put it at your disposal.'

'Very good of you, Melanie. That's just like you. In your own house you begrudge every lump of sugar, but when it's something big, you are always ready to give. But I don't need it.'

'And that reminds me that the children and Franz have been enquiring after you.'

'Nice of them. Is he all right?'

'Perfectly. But he works too hard, as usual.'

'And the children?'

'Rudy likes it very much in London,' replied the Baroness. 'He is doing well altogether. His firm are very pleased with him. That's something to be grateful for.'

She sighed and looked into her lap.

'What do you mean, "that's something to be grateful for"?' exclaimed Richard Marek. 'As though you had nothing but trouble and worries. While in reality you have got all your family dancing round you like the flies round the jam. You are a goose, Melanie.'

She shook her head at him reproachfully and tucked the subscription sheet into her handbag.

'I have not signed yet.'

'How thoughtless of me, Ricky.' She handed the sheet back to him.

'But you see, it's not very easy for me, you can believe it. Things don't always work out well, as you know.'

'True enough.'

'And I cannot attend to everything myself, Ricky. I am overburdened with obligations, I don't have to tell you. Franz is the best of husbands, of course, but he is hardly ever at home. And when he is, he is too tired to help me. I have often wished, Ricky, you would do more for me.'

She got up from the divan and stepped to the window.

Richard Marek remained silent.

'I am not asking so much for myself,' said the Baroness lightly. She lowered her voice. 'I am really thinking of Hedwig.'

She paused and looked at him.

Her brother stroked his hair. 'What's the matter with Hedwig?' he asked suspiciously. 'Does she want another fancy dress ball and am I to get it up for her again? I'll do it with pleasure, you know that. The young people nowadays have no idea how to enjoy themselves. I'll be again something unimportant so that I can slip all over the place and keep things going. Like the orange seller I was last time. Don't you think I was awfully good as the orange seller? But Franz must not be allowed to cheat again. Ha! A lounge suit and on his face a scar drawn with red ink and says he is a lion-tamer off duty. No, we can't have that sort of thing going on, eh, Melanie?'

'Ricky, this is not the time of the year for a masked ball.'

'No. You are right. What was I thinking of?'

'But I was going to ask you a favour. Ricky——'

'Yes?'

'Why don't you bring Count Szalay to my house?'

'Ah.'

'Why don't you, Ricky?'

'Why don't you, why don't you? Did I say I would not? Did I say anything at all? Do you ever give me a chance to say a word? So this is the charity and the cause for which you are peddling? You are out for blue-blood now, are you? I must say, you are a clever woman, Melanie, which does not mean that you aren't a goose at the same time. Nightingale, I hear thy warbling. Not that you could ever sing, Melanie. But you understand. What a fool I was to sign for three hundred crowns. Silesian fiddlesticks indeed. If I had known I would have signed for a hundred and fifty and the remains to be delivered in so many pounds of Hungarian livestock.'

He rose and bending over his desk, he picked up a paper knife and set it spinning between his fingers, while his sister, very upright on the divan, looked from one corner of the room to the other with a suffering smile as though to convince the onlooker that she was being forced to listen to subjects which pained her greatly.

Richard Marek threw the paper knife on the desk with a violent clatter and glancing sideways, he saw to his regret that he had not startled her.

'Very well,' he said curtly. 'Thy will be done. That is, if the Count is willing to be introduced.'

'Now you are being ridiculous, Richard.'

'I may be ridiculous. No doubt I am to many people.

And thank God for it, because as long as one is ridiculous, one is harmless. But you – you are worse, Melanie. And where has it got you? The Baroness Kreslov will be at home from five to eight o'clock every Thursday and God be with her. But who else is with her? You make me laugh. Where are they, the Hohenlohes and the Nostitz and the Lobkowitz? And the Coloredo-Mansfeldts and the Thun-Hohensteins? Has ever any one of them set foot in your house? And you dare to say that I am ridiculous! All you have got is Steffi Smejkal who was born a Countess Privoklad and you've got her because she is *déclassée*. Your nearest tie with the aristocracy is your manicure wench who was the mistress of Prince Kraslav. And now you think Count Szalay will come running with his tongue hanging out of his mouth because you graciously invite him.'

In the ensuing silence his breath came heavily.

His sister dabbed her mouth with a handkerchief and averted her face.

'You will have tea, won't you, Melanie?' said Richard Marek mildly.

She nodded.

He went to the door, opened it and yelled: 'Joseph! Joseph! Report at once.'

'Why don't you ring for the man, Ricky? He will think the house is on fire.'

'He doesn't think. I don't pay him to think. And I like to shout. So I shout.'

'I know you are right in many things you said,' continued the Baroness. 'I have no delusions, believe me.'

'You never had, Melanie.'

'And because of it, I try to do everything for the best. I

66

cannot go any further myself, but Hedwig can. And there is no reason why she shouldn't – I think that is your man at the door. Come in!' she called with a kind voice.

Joseph entered, his head bent so deep over the tray that his sideboards almost disappeared in his neckcloth. Breathing carefully through his nose, he put his load on the table and began to arrange the tea things with reverent movements. He had his own ideas about a gracefully laid table and after having spread the brocade cover with a Toledo work cloth adorned with old coffee stains, he placed the sugar basin in the middle, as it was of silver and therefore superior to the rest, and then disposed the cups, jugs, plates and dishes in a circle around it, so that the small objects alternated with the large ones, irrespective of their use. An arrangement which was probably an expression of his sense of justice.

As soon as he had withdrawn, the Baroness got up, drew the cups to the edge of the table and began to pour out. 'As I was saying, Ricky. At least Hedwig. I am only thinking of her.'

'Of course you are. You can't marry him yourself, can you?'

'The older you get, Richard, the more your jokes are in bad taste. I am not asking much. And surely – you of all people should be keen to help me. I don't want to drag in the past. But your own conscience should tell you. After all, it is all for the best.'

'For Heaven's sake, Melanie, stop fiddling about and pass me the tea. It's all for the best. You mean, it's the way you want it. I'll only tell you one more thing. There is no money there. Absolutely none. That is, as far as I know.'

'I am not concerned about it.'

'Very soulful of you, I must say. I did not know it was so difficult to get rid of the girl.'

'There is no question of that. For the past years, she has been rejecting offers right and left.'

'You mean you did, Melanie.'

The Baroness remained silent and stirred her tea.

'Have something to eat, Melanie,' said Richard Marek. 'I know, I know. I have been a disgrace to you with Sophy. But remember, you hurt yourself falling downstairs, but you can also get hurt falling upstairs. There is such a thing.'

He took out his handkerchief and blew his nose.

'Try some of the cherry cake, Melanie. Go on, have some – just to show that there are no hard feelings. I don't know what came over me, sitting here and playing the oracle of Delphi.'

She cut herself a small slice and ate it, standing.

'It's very nice, Ricky,' she said. 'It's mother's recipe.'

He was not listening. He rose, stroked his hair and looked dubious.

'There is something funny about this, Melanie. Has it occurred to you?'

'What, Ricky?'

'You came to see me yesterday, didn't you?'

'Yes.'

'With the same thing in mind, didn't you?'

'Yes.'

'So you knew already yesterday that Count Szalay was about. But I didn't. I was out when he called. And he called only after you had left. How did you know? You are not a fortune teller, are you?'

'I had heard about him the other day. I did not meet him, of course. But a friend of mine mentioned him. She asked me if I knew him because it appears that he is an old friend of yours.'

'Curse the woman! How did she know? How could she know? How could she know, I ask you? Why can't people keep their mouths shut?'

'I don't see why you are so annoyed,' said the Baroness. 'You talk as though it were a disgrace to be a friend of the Count.'

'Annoyed? I am more than annoyed. I don't like it, Melanie. I don't like it at all. I knew the old man in my Army days when I was billeted there. And the present Count was only a child then. So how could he know that I am I until he had seen me? I mean, that I am that same Richard Marek? I might be anybody for all he knows. He has not seen me yet but he already goes about in the cursed drawing-rooms of your cursed friends, and uses my name as a passport. Don't you understand? It puts a queer complexion on the whole thing.'

'You are making a fuss about nothing, Ricky. He arrives in Prague, a stranger. What could be more natural than to reclaim old acquaintances?'

'One does not go about it in that way.'

'He seems a very charming man, from all accounts. And who are you to——'

'You mean beggars can't be choosers, Melanie?'

'If you wish to put it that way.'

'But I am not a beggar, I tell you. I don't want anything from anybody. Still, do what you want. You know what you are doing.'

'I am glad that there is at least one thing about which we agree,' replied the Baroness kindly. 'And now, I must go. It has done me good to have a talk with you again, Ricky. Thank you for the lovely tea. It was so nice to eat that cherry cake again, after all those years. I believe it was as good as during the parents' lifetime, even if it was perhaps not quite so smooth as it used to be.'

CHAPTER 10

IT WAS a week later, in the afternoon. The tall clock in the hall emitted whirring and creaking sounds as it was getting ready to strike five, when the Kreslovs' car drew up in front of Richard Marek's house. As soon as the first faint and metallic thunder announced the hour, Anton stood in the hall in his newest fawn livery and fresh white gloves.

A few moments later he was installed by the kitchen table, his cap nestling against the pots of chives on the window-sill, while the cook poured out two cups of bitter, heated-up coffee with a certain grim enjoyment. Through the half open window came the scent of acacia flowers and logs drying in the sun.

In the drawing-room, Count Szalay was standing by the window playing with his eyeglass, while Richard Marek filled the brandy glasses.

'Might as well occupy ourselves usefully, eh Ferdinand, while my cook is playing the siren with my sister's chauffeur?'

'I shall be only too pleased to drink to your cook's very best health, although I have never met the lady.' And the Count bowed slightly.

Richard Marek carried the glasses to the music cabinet. 'Drink up, Ferdinand, don't waste your time. Brandy is like oysters. One is nothing, you don't even know you've had it.'

They raised their glasses and drank.

'This is a real occasion for me,' continued Richard Marek. 'I have not been out and about for such a long time, I feel quite a changed man. And now the changed man must have another glass of brandy.'

He refilled his glass and tossed it off at one gulp.

'Ah, that's better! I can highly recommend it, Ferdinand. I feel quite brave now.'

He lit a cigarette. 'You see, the thing is, that I have been keeping very quiet for the last few years. For one thing, my wife died, as I told you the other day, and I got a bit out of touch altogether.'

The Count nodded.

'But even before then – I might just as well tell you – it was a bit awkward for me. I did not mind really. But I often wished women were more like horses – you see your horse when you want to see it, and then you shut it up in the stable when you've had enough of it. You don't trail it with you, round to parties and all day long, if you see what I mean.'

The Count looked down at his feet with one eyebrow raised high.

'Stage?' he asked. 'Or the stage of life?'

'Bit of both. But she was a better actress off the stage than on.'

'I often think,' said the Count, 'what a pity it was that the Turks did not come to Vienna after all. They brought us the coffee and the coffee houses, that was one of their noble deeds, but if Prince Eugen had not beaten them, we would

72

have all gone Turkish and they would have bestowed their other blessings on us.'

'Ha! You are right, Ferdinand. And then I could have married Sophy and the whole chorus of the Prague theatre besides, and still dined out every night without having to blush.'

After they had both finished their brandy, Richard Marek wiped away two small tears which the sting of the liquor had brought to his eyes, and then motioned his guest to get ready.

'Anton should have had a nice chat by now and a nice cup of coffee. I think we will be cruel and tear him away from his Circe, what do you say, Ferdinand? First you very kindly offer to come here, so that the car does not have to fetch you separately and, instead of saving time, Anton goes and flirts in the kitchen. But it's always like that. If you try to save, you lose. Joseph! Joseph! We want to go now. Tell Anton that his halcyon days are over. The beautiful days of Aranjuez are past. How does it go? Where does it come from, Ferdinand?'

'*Don Carlos.*'

'May be. I am becoming very irresponsible with my quotations, Ferdinand. I think it is a sign of old age. And besides, I never know where the poet stops and Marek takes over, so to speak. I am making up an amazing amount myself, and sometimes I give myself surprises. And that's not as it should be, Ferdinand. That's always a bad sign. Ah! here they are, our gentlemen. On our way, Anton, or my sister will think – well, what will she think? Damned if I know. Fall back there, Rollo. Take the animal, Joseph, you sheep's head. And Anton, take us the way over the

Stephans Bridge. It's longer but it's prettier. I want to show Count Szalay the summer castle of Queen Anna up on the hill. The Count saved you time, so we've got to reward him, haha.'

Joseph remained under the porch until the car had rolled out of sight. Then he returned to the kitchen with the spaniel, who gave a half-hearted whimper from time to time.

The cook sat on the bench by the stove with her powerful red arms crossed over her breast.

'The Count comes here so that Anton won't have to go out of his way to pick him up,' said Joseph. 'I've never heard anything like it in my life.'

'You've heard it now. It's that he is considerate. Hark at the dog fretting.'

'If he stayed at the Esplanade or the Grand Hotel, he would want to be fetched. But he lives somewhere, where he does not like to be found out, take my word for it. His kind is no more considerate than a bed bug.'

The cook rose and gave him a fierce look from beneath her thick eyebrows.

'Seeing that I've never had bed bugs, I can't say. Did the master lock away the bottle?'

'No. He forgot.'

'Bring it here then. Anton's wife is in hospital and when I think of what he told me, I feel queer all over.'

She looked at the dog who stood by her feet and whined. His square, hanging cheeks and ears trembled with emotion and the whites of his eyes rolled mournfully.

'I'll soon stop your mouth,' she told him with that threatening expression which usually accompanied her kindest actions. Then she fetched a bone out of the stock pot and waved it in the air to allow it to cool, so that the cartilage glittered like mother of pearl.

'Now you get down to it and crunch it,' she said to the dog, as he received the bone from her hand. 'If you bite on it hard, it will give you a headache and when you've got a headache, it keeps you quiet.'

CHAPTER 11

MR. SIMEK was not a stranger in the house of Baron Kreslov. Like all good chefs he was as vain as a primadonna, as sensitive as a mimosa and as easily roused to anger as a turkey. From June to September of every year he directed the kitchen of the Hotel Royal in Karlsbad.

But in the winter months he led a life similar to that of a famous actress – he rested. And in between his rests he was willing – although reluctantly, if one was to believe him – to give what may be called 'guest performances' in the houses of the wealthy.

Although he was not tall, his bulky and inflexible figure seemed to tower in the kitchen larger than life size. His features were fat and crudely shaped, his eyes small, black, and unpleasantly intelligent. When he moved across the room with his waddling and yet dignified gait, while his flat cap flopped up and down and his white apron billowed around him, he looked a picture of ease and jollity.

Although he was a bachelor, he was blessed with a large number of relatives who were in the habit of paying him visits to break the monotony of his work. Invariably they carried large black wax cloth bags which looked empty on their arrival and stuffed to bursting point on their departure;

a regrettable manifestation of the family spirit which was greatly deplored by Fräulein Lotte. Yet she could do nothing to prevent it.

If Fräulein Lotte had possessed more wisdom and less sense of duty, she would have spared herself many a humiliation. As it was, she forced herself to 'look after things' on the mornings of the at homes of the Baroness, and if her experiences were varied they were never pleasant.

There were rare occasions when the chef was in a specially good mood and as soon as the housekeeper was seen in the kitchen he waddled over to greet, to acclaim, to honour her.

'That's what is so fine about our Fräulein Lotte,' he would say. 'That's what I like. She does not just eat what we send up. No, she takes an active interest in our cooking.'

'Yes, yes. Quite so,' replied Fräulein Lotte in despair and tried to brace herself to ask for the order sheet, while her long earrings dangled dismally round her faithful face.

'There is a little something I want to show you,' continued Mr. Simek and led her firmly to a side table. His expression was that of a benevolent nurse who prefers to be pleasant but will stand no contradiction.

'This is my latest creation, *Poudding aux profiterolles*.' The chef pronounced the words ringingly and in the French way, while the housekeeper found herself arrested by his arm and irritated by his flapping cap and looked with venom on the two rows of custard shapes on the table in front of her.

'Very pretty, no doubt about it,' she said with an oppressed voice, 'but I have been wondering if I could check the number of chickens and pheasants for to-day with you. It seemed to me rather a lot, considering——'

77

'Just what I thought,' exclaimed the chef and sounded overjoyed. 'I knew this would please our Fräulein Lotte. But this is not all.'

He lowered his voice: 'We must not judge by appearances, he, he! The proof of the pudding is in the eating. Ha, ha! He, he!'

Suddenly he straightened up and yelled over his shoulder: 'A knife! Lizzie, Berta, Marta, a knife! For our Fräulein. And get a move on. Our Fräulein has other things to do than to twiddle her thumbs in the kitchen.'

'Now,' he said, rubbed the knife on his sleeve and cut the pudding slowly. The layer of custard, about an inch thick, fell apart and revealed a crisp, cockled éclair. The éclair also was split and shown to contain strawberry cream.

'That's the success of my creations,' explained the chef to the pained-looking housekeeper. 'The element of surprise. You look at it and you think you know what to expect. Custard through and through. But let me cook for you and you will never get bored. It's not enough to feed – one must also entertain. He, he! We know what it is all about. Don't we, Fräulein Lotte? We know. We know,' and he took her arm and led her to the swing doors.

'Good cooking means good psychology. Ha, ha! We know,' he shouted after her, until her long, black-robed figure was out of sight.

'You've got to know how to handle the old battle axe,' said Mr. Simek to a scullery maid and he continued to look fondly through the door.

'And,' turning round majestically, 'we will serve it with raspberry sauce.'

Very rarely the Baroness herself appeared, walking with

slow and mincing steps over the tiled floor, closing her eyes and holding her head in her hands from time to time, thus indicating that for natures like hers the slippery floor and the incessant clanging, clattering, and banging which issued from the scullery, was a strain beyond endurance. 'I have been thinking,' she said, 'people may get tired of the eternal venison. And the salmon. Perhaps we could have a saddle of veal for a change and a carp in aspic.'

'Of course, if the Baroness wishes it. It would be much cheaper.'

The chef was a past master in the art of addressing people in the third person, which was really very servile, and yet managing to make it sound like an impertinence.

'That was not what I was aiming at, Mr. Simek.'

'Of course not. The Baroness does not to have to tell me that, it's just thoughtless of me. Now then, in that case we'll have a nice saddle of veal, carve it in slices and put between every two slices a sliver of smoked tongue and of *pâté de foie gras*, spread the whole with a Bechamel sauce and mushrooms, and brown it in the oven. That's much more interesting than venison and quite plain.'

The Baroness realised after a quick calculation how expensive the 'plain veal' would be. So she begged the chef to leave the menu unaltered, but made a suggestion about a sweet dish called 'tree-trunk', a confection of sponge cake and jam which was covered with whirls of chocolate cream and coffee butter so as to resemble the bark of a tree.

'The parents used to like it,' she added softly and gave him a wistful look.

'Ah! now, the Baroness does not have to tell me this. It's such an old fashioned dish – with all reverence to the

79

Baroness's parents, that I can hardly remember it myself. It is so out of date that it takes a very brave lady to put it on the menu. But we will make it. What wouldn't we do to please our Baroness? We will risk it. Because, as far as we can remember, it is a very heavy sweet. Cloyingly sweet, isn't that so?'

After having delivered this speech which was a double insult, he cocked his head to one side and beamed good will and devotion.

'And I always feel,' he added, dropping the royal 'we', 'that the tree-trunk is so much like the older generation. It's a cake made up to look like a tree, it's make-belief like everything else they practised. With all respect of course, to the Baroness's parents. Modern cooking is not so deceitful. But my goodness, here I stand, prattling on, never thinking of the Baroness's precious time. It's wicked. I am a wicked man, as true as there is a God in Heaven.'

With this he bowed as deep as his bulk would allow him and retreated into the idyllic coolness of the still-room, while the Baroness stood and looked after him with her slightly bulging blue eyes.

CHAPTER 12

'YOU WILL SEE that my sister is at home to so many people, that you will hardly catch a glimpse of her,' said Richard Marek to Count Szalay, as they emerged from the cloakroom and entered the hall.

Groups of people, talking and laughing, stood in the doorways which led into the reception rooms, and the palm trees and the low-hanging chandeliers barred a further view.

The hall itself was empty but it was filled with the droning hum of voices which seemed to come from various distances, from the adjoining rooms and also from rooms very far away, so that Richard Marek had to speak louder than usual to make himself heard.

At the head of the broad staircase stood a young girl of fourteen. Her blonde hair, falling straight round her small, white face, was cut short and tied on one side with a blue ribbon. Her gown was of pale blue silk and the skirt, with its numerous rows of frills from the waist to the ankle, was reminiscent of a crinoline. She wore white cotton stockings and sandals of black shiny leather. It was obvious that her dress was intended to be deliberately out of fashion and childlike.

She waved her hand and descended the stairs with a slow composure which was rather pathetic.

'Ah, here comes the first instalment,' said Richard Marek. She advanced gravely.

'This is a friend of mine, Count Szalay. Count Szalay, my niece Alexandrine.'

She inclined her head and extended her hand without speaking. 'And how is school, Ali?'

She dropped her left hand, which till then had rested demurely on her skirt and stepped from one foot on the other.

'We've got a lovely new teacher for natural science, Uncle Ricky. And he is awfully smart. He had on a dark green suit yesterday and a pale green silk shirt and a dark green tie and a green silk handkerchief. He is much too good to be an ordinary teacher, and he is secretary of the Jockey Club.'

The Count raised one eyebrow and smiled his curious inward smile.

Richard Marek guffawed. 'Ali, you are a goose,' he said. 'His get-up sounds ghastly. Eh, Ferdinand?' and he exchanged glances with his companion. 'Now I'll tell you something for life. A decent man never wears coloured handkerchiefs, he wears plain white ones. And he does not wear his handkerchief for show, he blows his nose in it. Jockey Club! He probably does the accounts for them there or something. Now tell me. Is your father about?'

'He has not come home yet.'

'He is a wise man. It sounds like the tower of Babel in there. It's no good asking you where your mother is, and Hedwig, I know that. It's like looking for a needle in a haystack. How many people are fighting for their food to-day?'

'There are always about three hundred people on Thursday,' said Alexandrine with a mixture of pride and resignation.

'Your mother believes in hard work, Ali. Well, I think we had better go in. I daresay you are going to worm your way through to the ice cream, eh?'

'I am not supposed to, Uncle Ricky. It spoils my supper if I do.'

She raised her skirt with her fingertips and smiled politely.

As she turned away, she was approached by a large, red-faced woman wearing a silver turban. 'Alexandrine,' she cried. 'And so grown up. I can hardly believe it! A lady, upon my word. Do you know who I am? You won't remember me, but I used to know you, when you were so high.'

Richard Marek watched his niece as she curtsied with childish decorum and then, shaking his head, he took the Count's arm and led him away.

'It's no joke, growing up in a rich house,' he said.

The Count played with his eye-glass and gave him a side-long glance.

Card tables had been arranged in a room upstairs, but the five main reception rooms were on the ground floor and disposed alongside the hall in a straight line. They were separated by folding doors and curtained archways and on a big reception day like this, when doors and curtains were flung open and offered endless vistas of scrolled mirrors, gilded settees, palm trees, marble statues and Venetian glass chandeliers, it was impossible to say how many rooms there were and where one ended and the other began.

As the middle space of the rooms was filled with clusters

of standing people and as the space round the walls was occupied with chairs and sofas on which nobody sat, Richard Marek and the Count made slow progress.

'Hold on, Ferdinand,' said Richard Marek. 'As I can't see anybody of the living family yet, I might just as well introduce you to the dead ones. And while I am pretending to explain them to you, we can turn our backs to the crowd and draw a few peaceful breaths. And I can relax my face – it positively hurts me from all the smiling. You can afford to laugh at me, Ferdinand. You are a stranger here and you look through them and above them, and if you seem sulky, so much the better. They'll think you are somebody important.'

With this they halted in front of two oil paintings, lifesize portraits of an elderly couple. He, small and bald-headed with blue hanging cheeks and mild, watering eyes, in morning dress and a ribbon in his buttonhole, with a rolled up document in his hand. She, a square-faced woman with greying brown ringlets, a naïvely upturned nose and red cheeks. The low-cut white satin dress framed her plump neck and shoulders which were still smooth and white. She held a fan in her hand, and a blue sash was tied across her breast in such a way, that it could have been mistaken for an order.

'The first Baron and Baroness Kreslov, as they looked when they were newly born,' said Richard Marek to his companion. 'Just managed to squeeze in five minutes before midnight, so to speak.'

The Count stuck his eyeglass under his brow and contemplated the picture with the cool amusement of a man who finds things to turn out exactly as he expected them.

'Better late than never,' he replied reasonably.

'It's all very well for you, Ferdinand. You can afford to be kind and tolerant. But I often curse them. Everybody to his own bad taste, of course, but only as long as it is not ridiculous. When the old man was made Commercial Counsellor, that was all nice and befitting and there he should have stopped. If one has lots of money, one should squander it, in a decent way of course, and when one has so much that one can't, then one should have it and be discreet about it. But building orphanages in places which would be better without them, that's not being decent, Ferdinand. And in the end the old Emperor has to hit back and create him a Baron and what good did it do then, I ask you? When you say Kreslov, people think sawmills and timber and then they think Baron and then they smirk. Now I suggest we wend our way past the curtain and if we show some courage and initiative we will eventually come to the dining -room.'

The dining-hall, chill and solemn with a coffered ceiling and tessellated marble floor, was filled with an embarrassing air of spirituality which was all the more pronounced as it formed a painful contrast to the false gaiety of the preceding rooms, with their curls of gilt wood and scrolls of silvered glass.

The walls were hung with vast Gobelin tapestries, woven in dusty greens and blues, with an intricately intertwined pattern of leaves and branches, of deer, hares and squirrels. Beneath the icy fire of the cut-glass chandeliers, the table, clothed in the stiff folds of white damask, and laden with a symmetrical array of dishes and flower-filled jardinieres, looked like an altar set with sacrificial offerings.

Fräulein Lotte officiated with capable and rather masculine gestures in front of a sideboard with a silver tea urn; when she was not busy with the cups, her eyes followed the movements of the maids and footmen who were constantly replenishing the stacks of plates and cutlery on the two side tables.

Although the room was lined with chairs, they seemed to be more of symbolical than of actual value, for all the guests, including the elderly, were standing or walking about in groups or couples.

Richard Marek looked round. In front of one of the windows, leaning against the sill, stood Steffanie Smejkal surrounded by several men. She held a glass plate in her hand, from which she ate with quick and pretty gestures. She wore a black narrow dress into the belt of which she had tucked her long gloves. The aigrette of black osprey feathers which cascaded over the brim of her black velvet hat, trembled at every movement and cast flickering shadows across her face.

When she talked, her admirers listened to her with an expression of dog-like expectation, and when she paused they laughed with the breathless and choking laughter of people who have been exhilarated for a long time already, while she glanced at their flushed faces with that air of innocence and surprise that is so often assumed by persons renowned for their wit after they have delivered themselves of a joke.

'Stop digging about in your fruit salad, Robert,' she said presently to an egg-faced and dandified young man. 'You worry it like a terrier worries a rat. It makes me feel restless.'

'The fruit salad is a scandal,' he replied and continued to

turn over the slices of apple and banana with the assiduity of a scholar turning over the leaves of a tome.

'It's quite true,' affirmed another. 'The food is getting worse every time.'

'I have gone through my entire helping,' resumed the young man called Robert. 'And I have not found a single piece of pineapple.'

The others sniggered.

Richard Marek approached the circle.

'How are you, Steffanie? I kiss your hand. You are the first pleasant sight I have come across yet. How are you, gentlemen? No need to look at me like that, I shan't be in your way today. I did not come here for pleasure. Steffie, allow me to present Count Szalay.'

She raised her head with a frowning, preoccupied look as though trying to recall something to her memory. Then she smiled quickly and turned towards the newcomer. He bowed and remained like this for a while, waiting. But she did not extend her hand. Richard Marek hurriedly introduced the others.

'Have you seen Melanie anywhere?' he then asked.

'She is in the garden, plucking pineapples,' replied Steffanie. The others burst into howls of delighted laughter.

'What's the matter now?' asked Richard Marek, stroking his hair and wrinkling his nose.

'*Il ne faut pas tâcher de comprendre*,' murmured the Count.

The young man called Robert turned to him: 'Have you been here before, Count Szalay? You haven't? Then take a tip from me. Leave the caviar eggs alone.'

'Indeed?'

87

'What's wrong with them?' asked a short, stocky man with a fleshy, aggressive, and thick-lipped face, and wavy black hair. His name was Wallern and he was Press Attaché to the German Embassy.

'What's wrong with them?' and Robert's voice grew high and broke with indignation. 'The eggs are not scooped out and filled with it. The caviar is only put on top.'

'It's quite true. The food is getting scandalously bad,' said someone.

'And the caviar itself,' added the young man Robert. 'It's as black as shoe polish and scandalously small grained.'

'Don't tell me,' said Wallern. 'It does not worry me. I come from peasant stock.' And he beat his chest with a powerful fist.

'But Robert cares,' said Steffanie. 'His father used to thrash him when he would not eat up his caviar.'

She waited languidly till the laughter had subsided. Then she said: 'Wallern, you are one of the genuine people here, aren't you? You are a bit of a bore with your peasant stock, but at least you never hold back with your past. I think you will sympathize with me when I tell you what happened to me yesterday. I went into the Café Passage in the afternoon and in the foyer I met the proprietor, Mr. Cerny. I had not seen him for some time and we sat down together and talked. "Do you know why I am here in person?" he said. "I walk about and watch the entrance door because I don't want any woman of ill repute to enter." To which I replied: "And by the will of God, one is sitting beside you now."'

The company screamed with laughter with the exception of the Count who played with his eyeglass and looked with well assumed absentmindedness beyond Steffanie's quivering aigrette and into the recess formed by the third window, where a tall and white-faced young girl in a modest brown silk dress and two rows of seed pearls round her throat, was listening earnestly to an energetic and monumental looking old lady whose white hair hung in untidy strands round her head.

Then he turned to his companion with an enquiring glance.

'Yes, Ferdinand, we had better be on our way,' replied Richard Marek to the unspoken question.

'I kiss your hand, Steffie. And Robert – much obliged for your culinary guidance. And Wallern – I wish you a steady hand with the plough at the Embassy, or have they put you to milking now, ha, ha?'

With this they left Steffanie Smejkal's circle.

'Steffie is charming, but she does not always collect the best crowd,' he said apologetically.

'Canaille,' replied the Count.

'It's a pity really,' continued Richard Marek. 'You have not seen her at her best to-day. Ah, look! There is Hedwig, my eldest niece, over there with the old woman. I might have known! As I was saying, Ferdinand,' and he took the other's arm, 'it's a pity about Steffie. You see, she comes of such a really good stable.'

'Even the finest horse can go astray.'

'True, Ferdinand. But I don't want you to get a wrong impression of her. She went out of her way just now to shock you. I can't think why.'

'I can, naturally, because I am a stranger. And if she paints herself very black, then there is a hope that perhaps others won't. I know the type. It is – forgive me saying so – not

89

very interesting. First they live on their beauty and then on their past.'

All this the Count said in a very low voice and without looking at his companion, while he kept a thoughtful eye on the young girl in the brown dress, without giving the impression that he was contemplating her.

'The old woman is a singing teacher,' said Richard Marek. 'I always talk to her about singing. Because if I don't, she does. So at least I get my word in first.'

As they came nearer, they heard: 'It's difficult to explain. I always say – stand here and then sing as though your voice came from over there.' And the old lady flung her arms towards the ceiling, while her hair streaked white and dishevelled over her forehead.

'Hedwig!' exclaimed Richard Marek and he patted his niece on the arm. 'And Mrs. Hellstein. How is your voice?'

'I never had one and you know it perfectly well.'

He introduced the Count and then continued in a bantering tone: 'Even so, I am, as always, at your feet with admiration. You look remarkably well, madam. I am overjoyed to see it.'

'I am never well. I can't be,' she replied vehemently. 'People of my type never are. We give ourselves and spend too freely. I am a flame which devours itself.'

'Mrs. Hellstein has a wonderful vitality,' said Hedwig with an embarrassed smile.

'Yes, Hedy. But I am now a mere shadow of what I used to be. When I was young – you will find it difficult to believe – my friends used to call me the wild bumble-bee. Temperament! But it's still there. Even if I don't show it any more. I have learnt to control myself. Master yourself, master your voice, and you master life. Do you see that man over there? I must speak to him.'

She grasped Hedwig's hand and worked it violently up and down like the handle of a pump. Then she stepped back, described a circle with her arm and called: '*A rivederci!*' They looked after her, speechless, while she sped away like a mad priestess in pursuit of an infidel.

Richard Marek mopped his brow with a handkerchief.

Hedwig twisted her hands.

The Count offered her a cigarette and as he bent towards her with the light, their eyes met for the first time.

'Hedwig, I put Count Szalay into your hands. Treat him well, he deserves it. His father took mercy on me when I was a green young subaltern and wet behind my ears and I have never been quite so delightfully drunk since. You ask the Count, he will tell you about my escapades. And I rely on you, Ferdinand, to tell my niece about the old days. Of course, suitably edited, *pour jeunes filles*, that's understood, eh? And now Hedwig, I will leave you for a while. I want to see Melanie. Have you set eyes on her?'

'Mama was in the small drawing-room last time I saw her, Uncle Richard. And Father has not come home yet.' She caught her breath and added, in a desperate attempt to detain him: 'But don't you want to have some tea first?'

'No thanks. I can't be bothered. I'll have it later, when all the bumble-bees are out of the way.'

They were left alone. Hedwig Kreslov touched the pearls on her throat with a tremulous smile on her white face. She was as tall as her mother but her figure was slimmer and her bones more finely made. She carried herself in a rigid, self-conscious way. Her dark, reddish brown hair was arranged in flat waves in a style too sedate for her twenty-two years. Her profile was immaculate, with her nose continuing the forehead in an almost straight line, reminiscent of Greek statues and this, together with her bloodless skin, lent her that pure and somewhat anaemic beauty which is always praised by women and avoided by men. Her eyes were soft and brown and most of the time her countenance was grave and slightly apologetic.

She turned to the Count, who watched her with that indulgent patience which one displays when listening to the utterances of a child.

'May I give you some tea now, Count Szalay? And perhaps I can interest you in some of the things on the table?'

'Please don't, Miss Kreslov. You will be doing your duty magnificently if you just allow me to keep you company for a while.' And he took her hand and kissed it with the easy and non-committal elegance which he showed in all his movements.

She coloured.

'Unfortunately, I have nothing much to recommend me as a *causeur*, none of that – what you were good enough to call wonderful vitality – of madam the singing teacher. Are you taking lessons with her?'

'No. I never learnt to sing.'

'Your mother does not approve of it, I daresay?'

'No. Mama is not musical. None of my mother's family is.'

'And so you are not allowed to be fond of music either. And the Baron? Don't tell me. I know. He would quite like it, if he ever had time for it. Isn't that correct?'

She looked at him with a bewildered smile.

The Count continued: 'You see, I have not met your parents yet. I only met your sister Alexandrine. She is what people call a sweet child. And that's just the trouble. She is trained and dressed to look like a sweet child and in a few years' time she will be promoted to a charming young girl and do the honours of the house and offer tea to strangers and rack her brain what to say next.'

Hedwig bowed her head while he gave her a quick side-long glance in which amusement was blended with calculation.

'Forgive me. But I know it all so well. You remind me of my sister. Although she threw it up and retreated from the battlefield.'

'Oh. Is she——?'

'No. She is not dead. She married somebody of whom nobody has ever heard and went to live in San Francisco. The climate there is very good, I am told. Let us hope so, anyway.'

'I am sorry,' murmured Hedwig.

'She used to amuse me, when she was about your sister's age, or a bit younger. Of course, when I say amused – I could afford to be because it is always easier for boys to get away from home; first school and then Military Academy and so on. We had a main staircase in our house, like yours, but higher and narrower. And when there were guests, my sister used to stand on the top landing and spit down on the bald heads of the men below.'

'How wonderful,' said Hedwig slowly and with a grave air.

'No, not wonderful, Miss Kreslov. But what is wonderful, is that you think it wonderful. If you had just laughed

93

and found it entertaining, I would have despaired of you. And if I dared, I would kiss your hand again but the lady over there – your uncle called her Steffie – is watching us and I am sure she would report it to the Baroness and denounce me as a bad influence.'

'Mrs. Smejkal? Never. She would be the last person in the world to do so. She is not in the least bit narrow-minded.'

'You are delightful, Miss Kreslov. I wish I could be as charitable as you are, but unfortunately I have seen too much of people. This Mrs. Smejkal, I cannot say that I had the honour to meet her, nor will I say I had the pleasure. I met her – *tout simplement* – a few minutes ago. And I can assure you that she would be only too quick to pounce upon any, shall I say, compromising conduct? She herself is not "narrow-minded", as you call it. She trades on it and makes it her claim to distinction. And just because of it she would not tolerate any competition. The same as Madam the singing teacher, would not suffer anybody to out-bumble-bee her.'

They looked at each other. Hedwig shook her head and laughed in that hectic and slightly desperate way which betrays a momentary relief from nervous tension.

Again the Count watched her, carefully, thoughtfully, and twisted the ribbon of his eyeglass between his fingers.

In front of them the throng of people who constantly changed their position, broke away from each other, re-grouped themselves, bowed, laughed and bent towards each other, surged incessantly to and from the enormous table which, monumental and white in the rigid folds of its drapery, stood like a rock lapped by the waves of a restless sea.

'There is Mama,' remarked Hedwig and her hand closed tightly over the pearls on her throat. Her eyes were troubled again as she turned to the Count with an embarrassed smile. It seemed as though she was regretting their previous frank conversation and imploring him not to continue on the same lines.

He understood. With one eyebrow raised and with his peculiarly inward smile, as though enjoying a secret joke, he said: 'I am willing to discuss anything you choose to think proper, Miss Kreslov. I have not been to the theatre yet, nor have I read the book of the moment. But I have a very effective way of saying: the play was rather weak, of course, although the production pulled it through, no doubt about it. And the book – well, very competently written, I thought. But no substance. None whatsoever. And that main figure in it. Then I pause and you supply the name. Ah yes. Very unconvincing, in my opinion. Or perhaps you would prefer something more homely and infallible? Do you like cheese, madam? Yes. Does your father like cheese? No. Does your mother like cheese? Yes. Does your cousin like cheese? I have not got a cousin. If you had a cousin, madam, would he like cheese?' Hedwig pressed her hands together and struggled with her rising laughter. And as her mother, followed by her uncle and old Professor Surovy, came towards her, her face bore the guilty flush and her eyes the moist sparkle, produced by suppressed merriment.

The Baroness advanced with her slow and commanding step, with her head cocked to one side and both arms slightly raised in front of her.

Her thick grey hair was dressed with dignified simplicity and was swept back so as to reveal her diamond and sapphire earrings. A long rope of large pearls fell over the coarse-grained and reddened skin of her throat and was tied into a knot over the triangular strip of Brussels lace which covered her mature bosom, and then dangled in a loop to her waist, where it touched a diamond clasp, fastening the belt of her dark blue silk dress.

Her countenance expressed surprise and pleasure.

She took another step forward, while the two men fell behind.

'Count Szalay?' she asked with a low voice, the inflection of which seemed to say: 'Is it possible?'

And then she repeated, as though answering her own question: 'Count Szalay', with an expression of: 'At last.'

While he kissed her hand, she continued: 'There is no need for introductions. I feel that I have known you for years, I assure you, and now that I have met you, you must allow me to express the great pleasure it gives me.'

Then with a movement, as though to sweep away any possible protestations on the Count's part, she added: 'My brother's friends are my friends, dear Count, and it fills me with great satisfaction that I can at last repay some of the wonderful hospitality which your family has shown Richard in the past. My only regret is that I shall never be able to thank your dear father for all his kindness to my brother. Richard has told me so much about him. What a very remarkable man! And your brothers – Richard told me. Don't say anything, dear Count. There is no need for words. I, too, have lost – life is never the same afterwards.'

And she closed her eyes for a second and pressed her lips together in a mask of pain, which she used when she wanted to express grief. Like most people who are frequently ex-

96

posed to the public eye, actresses and great ladies alike, she had acquired a number of gestures and facial expressions which denoted certain feelings in a manner more symbolic than real.

The Count bowed his head silently, Hedwig looked into space and twisted her pearls, while Richard Marek and Professor Surovy exchanged a glance as though to say: 'What next?'

The Professor was a painter and had been directing for many years, the Academy of Art. He was at home in many of the houses of the wealthy manufacturers and bankers of Prague and was responsible for a considerable number of the oil paintings which hung in their drawing-rooms.

He was a tall and upright old man of nearly seventy with neat, distinguished features, a small, white, pointed beard and tired eyes behind gold-rimmed pince-nez. With his urbane bearing and his precise and considered voice he seemed more like a high State Official than an artist, and it was probably this quality which was the reason for his social success, as many people are flattered by an acquaintance with artists and yet afraid of their behaviour.

The Baroness rallied with a fine show of spirit.

'I see that my little girl has been keeping you company. I hope you were not bored, Count Szalay. She is rather serious. I am afraid we are all a trifle serious. I was just the same when I was a young girl. I daresay you will find us different from the delightfully gay-hearted people of your country. Your beautiful country.'

'Oh, come Melanie, we are not as bad as all that,' exclaimed Richard Marek. 'The Count isn't a gipsy or a fiddler either, you know. Do you think he expects us to break into a

97

Czardas in his honour or what? Although if we did, the Professor here would find us more picturesque. Don't you agree, Professor?'

The Baroness ignored this. 'Allow me,' she said, 'Count Szalay – Professor Surovy.'

Then, while the two men turned to each other, she gave her daughter a quick and severe glance and drew herself up to her full height. Hedwig knew the signal. It meant: 'Keep your shoulders back.' And she straightened up with a guilty smile.

'I agree with the Baroness, agree with reluctance,' remarked the Professor. 'As far as one dares to generalize, it must be admitted that we are somewhat heavy and thick-blooded in this part of the world. A bit given to melancholy and brooding, I should say. You only have to listen to our Bohemian folk songs and you feel like drowning yourself.'

'And how does that affect painting?' asked the Count. 'I should be most interested to hear. Miss Kreslov and I were just discussing art a few minutes ago.' And he exchanged a glance with the young girl which brought a flush to her face.

'Ah, my dear Count, there you are touching a very sore point indeed,' replied the Professor and brought his spread-out hands together so that the finger-tips touched.

'Our art is a sorry business. The Slav soul is always in revolt, there you have our tragedy. We admire the form – the severe classic form. We are in love with it, if I may say so, we cast our eyes to Paris and to Italy and flirt with their formalism. We try to imitate their form and while we do so, we smash it. Smash it irretrievably.'

And the old man looked about him with a rueful eye, as

though searching for the broken bits of 'form' which one imagined to lie scattered over the carpet.

'You interest me,' murmured the Count, while the Baroness looked at him and the Professor with a vaguely pleased face, as though admiring a performance of which, although she could not follow it, she approved.

'Have you seen Steffie yet?' asked Richard Marek. 'She is in great form today.'

'In a moment, Ricky,' replied his sister.

She turned to the Count: 'It is so restful just to relax and chat for a while. Simple, friendly talk. You don't know how rare such moments are for me. The other day – I am almost ashamed to confess it to you – I was knocked down by a car. A stupid thoughtlessness on my part. The driver was not to blame, I assure you.'

And after a pause, in which she received the murmured distress of the company, she continued with her calm, measured tone: 'When I came home afterwards, I indulged in a great luxury. I lay down for half an hour. It was so beautiful to have a rest in the middle of the day. It was so beautiful, that I felt my little accident had been worth while.'

'Mama works much too hard,' said Hedwig. 'Father and I always tell her so.'

'I only do my duty, Hedwig. And I will never neglect my charities, whatever happens. My little girl is a great help to me, Count Szalay. The pressure on my time grows daily and without her I would not know how to manage. My son is away for the present, he is in London. But while I have Hedwig, I have all the support a mother could wish for.'

She gazed with fond pride at her daughter. 'Although,' she continued, 'I often reproach myself for making too many demands on her. She should get more distractions, more fresh air. I blame my brother, too. Forgive me for being so frank, but you have known Ricky for so long, you will understand. I had always hoped he would take the girls riding with him regularly – we keep a few horses in the Baumgarten, of course – but somehow it never happens. My dear brother is rather lax, I am afraid. Yes, Ricky, I have to accuse you of negligence. You will allow me to say so.'

'I am greatly honoured to be taken into your confidence, madam,' replied the Count. 'I am sorry to hear what you tell me, but not altogether surprised. The Major is such a magnificent horseman, of course, that it is a great pity if he does not impart his knowledge to others.'

'Fiddlesticks, Ferdinand. The girls have got a perfectly good riding master, an Englishman who used to be for years at Buckingham Palace. What more do they want, I ask you?'

'It is not the same thing, Ricky,' replied the Baroness with gentle reproach. 'There are so many angles to the question. A paid teacher does not care sufficiently. I was quite a good horsewoman myself once upon a time, so I know. I think the Count will agree with me.'

'Entirely, madam. And an Englishman, you say? I don't hold with their views; I never have. We had different ideas in my regiment. For instance the question of dressage, the English are lamentably backward with it and if I say backward, I am being very polite. They almost ignore it. A horse should be coiled up like a ball of string the whole time and firmly collected. And not be allowed to flop all over the place with head and legs all astray.'

'Quite true, Ferdinand. But then we go to the other

extreme. Our Spanish High School, for instance. Why should a horse dance a quadrille? God never meant it to. It's very cruel, I think.'

'It need not be cruel,' said the Count.

'You see how difficult it is to talk to my dear brother,' said the Baroness. 'This is true and this is not, but what does he do himself? Nothing at all.'

'You put me in a very delicate position, madam. Your brother is a superb horseman, as we all know, and this makes it still more difficult for me. I myself am quite passably good, of course; it would be hypocrisy on my part if I denied it, as it was part of my career. But even so, it might be taken for downright impudence if I offered my services. Indeed, I dare not do so.'

'My dear Count, you would relieve me of a great burden if you did,' said the Baroness. She clasped her hands and looked up to the ceiling, 'of course, I did not want to suggest it to you, it would have been an imposition. But as you said it yourself – you don't know how much it would mean to me. The Englishman is quite sound, I believe. But if you would just keep an eye on Hedwig, a little hint here and there. Style is so important in these things. As I said, you would be doing me a great service. And Hedwig will be delighted, won't you my dear?'

'You are too kind, madam. I am overwhelmed.' And the Count seized the Baroness's hand and kissed her finger-tips with such an air of exaggerated courtesy, that it was almost an insult.

'Ferdinand is a decent fellow,' shouted Richard Marek. 'He won't let you down, Melanie. He'll turn the girl into a circus rider before you know where you are, and she'll be dashing off the horse and picking up handkerchiefs with her teeth while the Professor and I will beat the drum. Isn't that what you want?'

'Not entirely, Ricky,' said his sister with a brilliant smile. 'Richard always makes fun of me, Count Szalay. But you understand my worries, I know you do. It is a great relief to find someone sympathetic. One's own family, you know how it is. No one is a prophet in his own country.' And she swept over the company a glance of gentle martyrdom.

'To come back to your distressing experience, dear madam,' said the Professor. 'I, too, had a similar accident about a year ago. What surprised me so much was my own reaction. There I lay in the street; I had a slight cut, but did not feel any pain. I looked at my blood mingling with the dust and kept thinking what a wonderful splash of colour it made. The red and the grey. I could not take my eyes off it, strange to say.'

'You are an artist, Professor,' replied the Baroness with great conviction. 'What it is to have such gifts as yours. We ordinary people – how dull we must seem to you. No, I assure you. I have often prayed to God. Prayed on my knees to give me more understanding of art.'

'It's not so difficult, Melanie,' said Richard Marek. 'One always knows what's nice and what isn't. When we were in Italy, Professor, I always said to Sophy, that's something, Sophy. And it always was something. Although perhaps. Well, I don't know.'

Hedwig, meanwhile, stepped near the Professor and plucked at his sleeve.

'Would it be all right now?' she whispered.

'Certainly, my dear young lady.' And in a louder voice,

with a slight bow and a round gesture, the old man continued: 'If you will excuse us madam, gentlemen? Miss Kreslov and I have a little secret errand. I think you can trust me, dear madam, with your daughter. My white hair speaks for me.'

The Baroness shook her head and laughed indulgently, while the Professor offered his arm to Hedwig with old-fashioned courtesy and led her away.

'Our little circle is breaking up,' said the Baroness wistfully. 'Have you had anything to eat yet, Count Szalay? My brother will look after you, I trust. If he does not, I shall be very annoyed with him. And you will come and say goodbye to me before you go? I rely on it. I have hardly had time to talk to you, dear Count Szalay. We shall leave it like this for for the present. Alas, I must be on my way now.'

And she moved away with a most cordial nod.

CHAPTER 13

As the hour progressed, the demand for tea slackened and Fräulein Lotte handed over her place by the tea urn to a footman. Then, like a general who surveys the battlefield, she made a tour of inspection round the big table. As usual, the dishes with the choice delicacies were empty, while the more commonplace viands had remained untouched.

The smoked salmon was gone and so was the *pâté de foie gras*; a few shreds of ham strayed pink and dishevelled round the bare bone and over the limp frill on the knuckle. Yet, amidst the litter of petals and leaves, of salted almonds, bread crumbs and lemon slices, the carp rested intact beneath its patterned mould of jelly, calm, solid and undisturbed in death as it had been during its lifetime, on the muddy bottom of the pond.

The remnants of the hazelnut ice-cream swam in a pool of brown liquid in the Dresden tureen and the two maids responsible for it dished out an insipid vanilla cream instead, and when they dipped into the boats containing the chocolate sauce, their ladles came up half empty.

The once proud pyramids of sponge fingers had crumbled beneath the ravages of greedy hands and the towering monumental cakes built up of elaborate tiers of pink and brown layers, whirls of whipped cream and chains of glacé fruit, were trailing their last sugared glory across the soiled silver.

Fräulein Lotte saw it, and, turning over in her mind the reserves of Russian eggs, smoked tongue and sweetmeats, she hurried into the kitchen.

She found Mr. Simek in the dreamy coolness of the still-room where he chopped aspic and selected sprigs of parsley with the determined air of a man who does his task grudgingly, but is prepared to see it through.

'We must have more chocolate sauce,' she said nervously. 'And Mr. Simek, I have been thinking – the eggs in the green mayonnaise, they are still there, aren't they? They must be sent out at once.'

'My goodness. Fräulein Lotte is here. And I hardly noticed it. I never heard you come in. Who would have thought it? Is there anything we can do for you? We'll do anything to please our Fräulein.'

With these words the chef waddled beside her into the main kitchen where he stopped and yelled a few orders.

At once the platters were presented with the shiny rows of eggs and before they were dispatched, the chef sprinkled aspic over them like a last blessing of holy water.

'The sauce will be brought in a second,' he assured her.

'And what about the tongue, Mr. Simek? We could do with some. People are still arriving. The ham is finished. There is only the fish left.'

'Tongue? Did you say tongue?' asked Mr. Simek, and he shook his head in bewilderment so that his large, white cap flapped about his ears.

'There was some. I ordered it myself,' insisted Fräulein

Lotte and raised the knuckles of her clenched fists to her lips.

The chef without a word stepped behind the long carving table near the stove, gripped a meat knife and turned it slowly, so that it glittered grimly in his hand. He also very slowly rolled his sleeves up, looking all ready for action although there was nothing to carve. He then leaned across the grooved wooden surface with his arms bent like someone thirsting for a fight.

'Tongue?' he repeated with a pleasant voice, touched his sleeves belligerently and waved his awful knife. It was impossible to misunderstand him.

'It does not really matter,' replied the housekeeper in a tone of voice which gave the lie to her words. 'I suppose I made a mistake.'

'What's wrong with the carp, anyway?' asked the chef. 'Mind you, it's not a salmon, but whose fault is that? God made us the way we are. We are all His creatures.'

'Yes, quite,' breathed Fräulein Lotte, added a toneless 'thank you,' and sped away with shaking earrings.

Outside the door she almost collided with Hedwig and Professor Surovy.

'This is a pleasant surprise,' exclaimed the chef and advanced towards the visitors – a grotesque and yet dignified figure. He was the picture of benevolence.

'I brought you Professor Surovy,' said Hedwig fondly and shook his outstretched hand. The chef clasped her fingers in both hands and turned to the Professor.

'This is an honour, indeed. Professor Surovy in person! Who would have thought it? And our Miss Hedy. The sweetest little lady I ever saw. I go in many houses, Professor and I see many ladies, but none of them like Hedy. And the way she has grown up, so beautiful.' He paused and added with the voice he used when contemplating his own 'creations' in the oven: 'She is coming on wonderfully well. Miss Ali is growing up, too, but she will never be a patch on our Hedy.'

With a vivacity which she had not displayed before during the afternoon, Hedwig asked: 'And have you got them ready, Mr. Simek?'

'Of course I have. They are not up to much, Professor, merely a hobby, you understand. During the day I paint with mayonnaise and whipped cream and at night with oil colours, hehe.'

'Very interesting. I look very much forward to seeing your pictures,' replied the old man and adjusted his pince-nez.

'This is great day for me, a great occasion. Who would have thought it?' babbled the chef with charming artlessness. But his unpleasantly intelligent eyes rested on the Professor as though to say: 'You are somebody and so am I. We are each a king of our own calling.'

With a great deal of bustle which underlined in a flattering way the excitement he pretended to feel, Mr. Simek conducted his visitors to a sidetable and made them sit down after having swept the corner of his apron over two kitchen chairs. Then he left them.

'Extremely interesting,' remarked the Professor.

'Isn't it lovely?' asked Hedwig. 'So quiet and peaceful. I always feel so much at home here. Everything is so clean and inviting.'

'Yes, yes,' replied the Professor soothingly 'These rich

women,' he thought, 'the mother is in ecstasy when she can lie down for half an hour and the daughter adores the kitchen.'

The chef returned with an armful of canvases, which he hugged with the smile of a conspirator. He placed them one by one on the table. Hedwig and the Professor stood up and bent over them.

They were landscapes with blue and clouded skies, with flowering shrubs and grassy banks behind white palisading and gates, with gravel paths leading up to houses in the background.

'The perspective is not up to much,' murmured the chef.

'That is a great virtue,' replied the Professor. 'Perspective does not mean anything. It is one of our pointless conventions. The Chinese and the Egyptians ignored it and so did the Primitives and they achieved great works of art. There are much more important things to be considered. Your values are very nice. Very nice indeed. Look at this house, for instance. I must compliment you on it. You are successful exactly at a point at which most amateurs fail. A very considerable achievement. I am perfectly serious.'

'But the proportions – they get me down.'

'That does not matter either. The old Greeks did very well until they became conscious of proportions. In the end this spoilt their art. No,' continued the Professor, and lifted a picture and held it away from him with an outstretched arm, 'What you should watch are your colours. The cooler your colour, the greater your distance. And so on. Have you ever had tuition?'

The chef shook his head and spread out his hands with an emphatic gesture of regret.

'Amazing,' said the Professor and tapped with a crooked finger on a canvas. 'You have got a lot there.'

Then he took off his pince-nez, bent again over the table and, pointing to various parts of the pictures, he explained some of their shortcomings.

He was still thus occupied when the glass doors swung open with a clatter. Hedwig turned round with that glance of irritation and apprehension which people have when they are surprised during a not quite honourable action. But as soon she saw her father, she relaxed.

Baron Kreslov advanced with his small hands folded comfortably over his rounded stomach which was girt with an old-fashioned gold watch-chain. He was a small, dark man in the late fifties, short necked, broad and portly. His mouth and nose were small and well cut but they seemed blunted by the pasty expanse of his hanging cheeks and jowl. His eyes were deep-set and alert but their whites were discoloured and this, together with the baggy skin beneath them, gave them an expression of doubt and disillusionment.

'Is this how I find you?' he asked with his deep voice which sounded rumbling and good-natured at the same time. 'Have you all gone crazy or have I? The chef paints and the painter cooks and you, Hedwig, instead of propping up the walls in the drawing-room, sit about here idly as though a party was an excuse for malingering.'

'Oh, Father,' said Hedwig, and put her arms round his neck and kissed his cheek.

'The Baron is late,' said Mr. Simek. 'All those fine ladies and gentlemen have been here for hours already, but no Baron to be seen anywhere.'

'I had a board meeting,' replied Baron Kreslov. 'It must

have lasted for a long time, because I filled three large sheets with steps and little houses and profiles. I am a devil for profiles, Professor. Positively reckless.'

'Ah yes,' replied the old man absentmindedly and contemplated the paintings with one eye closed and his head resting on one shoulder.

'I have been wondering if I could have some bread and butter?' said the Baron. 'It is positively the only thing I can face. I'll have to go in sooner or later and so I thought I had better have a bite first. I cannot stand the sloppy mess they throw at you in the dining-room.'

'Can't say I blame the Baron. Still, what do you want? I've got to make a living, hehe. But never at the Baron's expense, no fear. A slice of bread and butter cut with my own hands. Lizzy! A plateful of bread and butter. And look sharp.' Then, with the condescending air of a busy man who forces himself to entertain an important visitor, although he would prefer to see him gone, the chef continued: 'There was nothing suitable for the Baron, in any case. Except the ham perhaps, and that's gone. The only thing left now is the jellied carp, hehe. And that I would not wish on to my worst enemy, haha. But it fills the table, hehe.' And holding his sides he burst into laughter, which made the others join in, although they did not see the joke.

'My God, the eternal carp, I positively respect it,' remarked the Baron. 'Yes, Simek, you laugh. But I am quite serious. The carp is a survival of the simple old days, when we regarded it as a delicacy, not to mention the Christmas carp. Now it's a fossilized institution which we dare not throw on the rubbish heap and yet we have no use for it any more. What a poor fish, I think and I feel positively sorry for him. I do. Really. And why do I feel sorry for him? Do I strike you as a sentimental undergraduate, Simek, who writes poetry, or a commercial traveller who cannot see a lilac tree in bloom without crushing a tear?'

'Heaven forbid,' replied the chef and folded his hands with an exaggerated look of fright.

'The carp makes me feel uncomfortable' said the Baron, 'because it reminds me of all that we have been. Thank you. That's fine. Just as I wanted it.'

And stuffing into his mouth the folded slices of buttered bread which the chef handed him in person, so as to indicate that he had cut the bread himself – if not in reality, at least in spirit – the Baron continued while the crumbs rolled down his chin and over his waistcoat: 'We have come up in the world and left the poor carp behind. We've got caviar now. Well and good. There is nothing wrong with it, I suppose? There is nothing to stop me from having whatever I want. And yet, it's not as simple as that. With one eye I squint at the caviar, though mind you, Simek, that's only a figure of speech and I would not dare to eat a mouthful of it, my stomach being what it is. Still, I want the caviar and yet I have the hypocrisy to put the carp beside it and to pretend that my life is as simple as that of my forefathers. It's rather disgusting, when you come to think of it. If I were a strong man, I would give the carp such a kick that it would roll down all the way into the Moldau. But I am weak, Simek. I only curse it and yet it fills me with awe.'

'Now, now,' said the chef. 'The Baron wants to curse it because he has a weak stomach, but otherwise there's nothing wrong with him. The Baron just feels a bit out of sorts today. We all do. Even I do, sometimes.'

'Do you really, Simek?' asked Baron Kreslov with a voice avid for confirmation.

'Certainly. And now I'll send for the carp and have it out of sight so that the Baron will not be upset when he gets to the dining-room. Would the Baron want any more bread?'

'No thanks, Simek. I feel fine now. You do me good. My God, if you knew what I suffer sometimes. The other day we had boiled beef and it took me positively two days to get over it.'

'Dear me. Who would have thought it?' replied Mr. Simek, crossed his ham-like arms and shook his head.

'Well, children, I suppose we had better be going,' said Baron Kreslov and his voice, which during the foregoing conversation had been tired and low, now resumed again its usual jovial and rumbling quality.

'Father,' said Hedwig, 'please ask Mr. Simek to cut an onion. The professor has only looked at the pictures. But he has never seen anything real yet.'

'Very well. Will you do it, Simek please?'

'Certainly. There's nothing to it. Who could not cut an onion? But for Miss Hedy I'll do anything.' And the chef waddled to the carving table.

A few moments later they crowded round him. He held a peeled onion between two fingers and slashed it with a knife so quickly that one could not follow his movements with any accuracy. Then he laid the knife aside, still holding the seemingly unchanged vegetable between his fingers and remained thus for a while in order to increase the growing tension. Suddenly his hand fluttered upwards and the onion broke into a myriad of minute cubes, all cut with a beautiful precision to exactly the same size.

'What a hand. What an eye!' exclaimed the Professor. He insisted on shaking hands with the chef and assured him of the genuine pleasure which the meeting had given him.

'The gentlemen must go back to their own pleasures now,' remarked Mr. Simek. 'And Miss Hedy, too. Or Madam the Baroness, will wonder what has happened.'

He beamed. He was a picture of benevolence. Immobile, grotesque and dignified, he remained on the spot, till the last echo of footsteps and voices had died away from the white-tiled walls.

'You go ahead, Hedwig,' said the Baron as soon as they had reached the hall, 'and tell your mother that I have come home.'

After she had left them, he drew the old man to a side-table whose fleshy pink and red-veined marble top seemed to grow out of the wall like an oversized tropical flower and on which stood the head of a youth sculptured in stone. The tip of the nose and some of the clustered locks had crumbled away.

'Is it any good?' he began to ask.

'Not really, dear Baron.'

'You mean it's not genuine?'

'Perfectly genuine, I should say. But it does not come from a good period, late Roman.'

'Melanie likes it,' said the Baron.

'It is rather unusual for ladies to show any real appreciation for sculpture,' said the Professor with a non-committal voice.

'And in its way, I mean in its late Roman way, you think it's quite all right?'

'It is a pleasant piece of furniture, dear Baron.'

113

'So you have no quarrel with it?'

'It is not a problematical piece and as such rather restful.'

After having thus delivered an opinion which could never be quoted against him, the old man looked round and said: 'There comes Mr. Smejkal. Who is the person with him?'

'Couldn't say. We'll find out soon enough.'

It turned out that Mr. Smejkal's companion called himself Maly and had come up from Pardubice for a few days.

'Mr. Smejkal was kind enough to bring me here,' said Mr. Maly and a sudden angelic smile appeared on his face. 'I have already been introduced to the Baroness. What a wonderfully charming lady! The real thing! I can always tell. Blood is stronger than water. And now I have the honour to shake hands with Baron Kreslov. I have to go soon and I was already afraid I would not be able to see you. I dragged Mr. Smejkal all over the place. Is that the Baron? Or that? I kept asking. But it never was. I almost despaired.'

'Much obliged. Very kind of you, Mr. Maly,' said the Baron.

'Don't say that. People always say I am kind. It is true, I suppose, but I wish they wouldn't. It embarrasses me when they say it. As I said, we could not find you anywhere. You work long hours, don't you? I can imagine it. You don't keep up all this with nothing.'

With parted lips, Mr. Maly looked at the lofty ceiling encrusted with gold, at the chandeliers dripping with their sparkling load of glass drops, at the distant walls, almost concealed by the dark and glossy screen of palms; and then, as all these splendours were out of his reach, he pointed to the floor at his feet, spread with a Persian rug which glowed in tints of spilled blood and wine.

'As it happens, we were just in the kitchen, the Professor and I,' replied the Baron.

The effect of his words was astonishing. Mr. Maly dropped both arms to his sides, threw his head back and laughed long and loudly, so that the Baron could see not only his beautiful small white teeth, but even his wholesome-looking tongue and palate.

Mr. Smejkal shrugged his shoulders, while the Professor looked absentmindedly into the ever-changing crowd of guests.

'What a wonderful sense of humour you have, Baron,' said Mr. Maly after he had recovered. 'And you looked so serious. You nearly took me in.'

'But I am serious,' replied Baron Kreslov. 'You think I am joking? My God, if one has a stomach as weak as mine, one does not make any jokes, I can assure you.'

He took the Professor's arm and after a short greeting they moved away.

'So you say that head is quite genuine?' asked the Baron as soon as they were out of earshot. 'You know, I got it from Rosenbaum, the gallery by the river. What you said about it, well and good. Melanie likes it and even if it is the wrong Roman period, why shouldn't she have it? There is positively no reason why she should not, is there?'

'It has certain merit, no doubt, dear Baron.'

'Glad to hear it. But this Rosenbaum, I don't know him from Adam and I am a business man first and foremost. He tells me it is genuine. Of course, he tells me that, it's in his interest to say so. But how do I know? What it costs is neither here nor there, money is no consideration. But I must know what I am buying that's how I look at it.'

'Rosenbaum is a most reputable dealer, dear Baron.'

'Reputable. That does not mean a thing. We are all reputable but it does not stop us from clinching a deal which is to our advantage. So I told him, I would take it on approval. I wanted you to see it. And so you are convinced it is all above board?'

'Definitely, my dear Baron. The best reason for my conviction lies in the fact which I have already told you. Nobody would counterfeit a sculpture in a style which is not in demand. One fakes only what is worth while.'

'Excellent. Now you have convinced me. Supply and demand – that's an argument which makes sense to me. Art and style and period – there I am a fish out of water. But from a business point of view, I can tell a good proposition from a bad one. And faking is a trade like any other. I see positively no reason why it should not be.'

He folded his hands above his watch-chain and, giving tired nods right and left, he walked by the old man's side in silence.

'I dare not stop,' he added after a while. 'Most of the people here – Heaven knows where Melanie gets them from! Still, as long as she knows. Why shouldn't she? This Maly for instance. Pardubice. That's not coal. And it's not leather. If Smejkal brings him, he should be in sugar, but in that case I would have known the name. Or perhaps it is one of the new refineries? Kapp and Horny folded up when the Union Bank in Vienna crashed. Perhaps he is the man who has taken over?'

'I am afraid there I can be of no help to you, dear Baron,' replied the Professor, who had been developing very similar calculations in his head. 'Unless he is in chicory. Chicory and sugar, they always go together. They meet in the coffee, so to speak.'

'Excellent. And do you know, I think you are right. You artists. You always see things from such a different angle. Haha, I must tell Melanie. Remind me to tell her. She will find it priceless.'

They were now in the second drawing-room. Two pairs of rosewood book-cases, framed in fluted pillars and crowned by triangular pediments, so that they looked like entrances to Greek temples, were disposed along the wall space between the windows and reflected in their latticed glass doors the bronze candelabra on black porphyry stands which were placed on the opposite side of the room. In each corner stood a black marble pedestal with a carved stone bust of a Greek philosopher.

Unfortunately, the air of the place which invited to serious thought and study was put to shame by the large number of French chairs and settees which, with their white and gilded frivolity seemed to have been introduced from a later and more shallow age.

'Queer *ménage*, the Smejkals,' said the Baron. 'He is very sound, mind you, all due respect. Though as a couple – I don't know – a racehorse pulling a manure cart, I should say. She is a beauty, all due respect again. But I never know what to make of her.'

'An eccentric lady, my dear Baron. A spoilt woman.'

'Yes. But what is she driving at all the time? Sometimes, when I talk to her, I have the feeling that she despises me, all of us, for that matter. The next moment she gives me the impression that she despises herself. And then her beauty. I don't know. The other day, I happened to stand close behind her at a concert and her ears were positively yellow. No freshness there, nothing appetizing. Ears are very important, don't you think?'

'Everything is important, dear Baron.'

'So it is.' The Baron paused and mused. 'You know, I have never been unfaithful to Melanie. I cannot say that I never had the inclination, but I always am afraid of her.'

His fingers touched some keys and coins in his pocket and made them jingle, while his eyes, so used to appraise and assess, swept round the over-crowded room with a mixture of contempt and resentment. 'To tell the truth——'

But Professor Surovy pressed the Baron's arm and, adjusting his pince-nez with an elegant, slow, and yet decisive movement of his old and well-kept hand, remarked: 'My dear Baron, there are occasions when one has to lie to tell the truth.'

CHAPTER 14

TWO HOURS LATER, at half-past eight, the main rooms on the ground floor lay in silent darkness. Only from time to time the wood creaked in the heat and groaned, or a curtain in front of the half-opened windows moved over the floor, so that it sounded like the swish of ball dresses. The brisk and somewhat damp air of the April night penetrated among the stale odours of tobacco, food and perfumes, flowers and wax polish.

The palms in the hall looked tired and deserted beneath the thin and yellow glow of a single lamp. Several folded card tables stood propped up against the foot of the staircase. Through the farthest of the now folded glass doors trickled dim lights and voices.

In the small drawing room the Baroness Kreslov stood exactly in the middle of the rose wreath which flowered on the pale Aubusson carpet. Her husband and eldest daughter leaned against the wing of the harpsichord. Above their heads a couple of wall sconces were still burning and each of their flame-shaped electric bulbs threw a golden halo on the wall behind it.

At the sound of footsteps, they all turned their heads to

the door and watched in silence as Fräulein Lotte came into the room.

'Come in,' said the Baroness.

She raised her arms, Fräulein Lotte stepped in front of her and took off her bracelets and the diamond wristwatch. The Baroness dropped her arms wearily and turned her neck to the housekeeper who unfastened the diamond and sapphire safety catch at the back. The pearls slid into her hollow palm where they rested like a whitish cluster of grapes. At last the Baroness inclined her head and her diamond and sapphire earrings were replaced by modest pearl studs.

'Has Alexandrine had her supper?' she asked. Her voice was so tired that it remained quite flat and did not rise at the end of her question.

'She had a nice egg and a nice rice in milk. I have sent her to bed now. Mademoiselle Bergot is reading with her for half an hour.'

'But lights out after that, do you hear, Lotte? The child needs her sleep. And tell Netty I'll be up in a few minutes and she can bring me a pot of marshmallow tea in the meantime. My voice is finished again, I can feel it, and by tomorrow morning I shall not be able to utter a word.'

'Goodness me, it won't be as bad as that? We'll put a nice spoonful of honey in the tea and madam's voice will be as clear as a bell and as smooth as glass. I'll go now and lock the things up and afterwards we can do a little gargling. Good-night, sir, good-night, Hedy.'

The Baroness had listened to the last words with a smile of polite disbelief like a mortally ill person who is too tactful to contradict his friends' assurance about his recovery.

'Thanks, Lotte,' she breathed with a dying voice, while Hedwig inclined her head and the Baron called a loud and rumbling: 'Good night, Fräulein.'

'Funny this,' he continued after she had gone. 'When I hear her talking the way she does about nice rice and nice spoonfuls and nice gargling, I feel as though I were five years old again. But why not? There is positively no reason why I should not feel it, is there?'

'Franz, please,' said his wife tonelessly and closed her eyes for an instant. She moved to the curved settee which stood against the wall behind her and sat down, holding herself very upright. Her arm rested on the back of cherry coloured satin and she tapped with one finger on one of the buttons which ran in several rows over the diapered quilting. She said with her commanding voice which had suddenly regained its usual strength: 'I must say, Hedwig, that I cannot understand you. Why must you always talk to old people? It is most unnatural in a young girl. Give me a reason for it, give me one reason, if you please. But you can't. You don't know yourself.'

She shook her head again and closed her eyes as though in despair.

'These receptions are given so that you should meet people, new people. Instead of which you go off with Professor Surovy. If I did not know you, I might believe you were doing it to spite me.'

'Take it easy, Melanie. She just does not like parties. I don't either,' remarked the Baron.

'Allow me to contradict you, Franz. They give you pleasure and if they don't, it is only because you are too tired to enjoy them,' replied his wife. 'But Hedwig has no excuse whatever. I was speechless at your behaviour, Hedwig, I think I must be allowed to say so. You meet a man who is distinguished and who goes out of his way to make himself pleasant to you, which is more than you deserve. And you got on so well with him, I observed you. Animated and laughing and then suddenly you retire with the Professor and without as much as a word. If the ground had split open beneath my feet, I would have gladly been swallowed up by it. I was so ashamed of you, I did not know what to say.'

'Who is this model of virtues, Melanie?'

'Count Szalay. Richard introduced him. You remember? We asked him to dinner for next Monday.'

'Did we? Glad to hear it. Is he the fair one with a monocle?'

'Yes. Now tell me, Hedwig, what made you do it? Didn't you like the Count?'

'I did Mama. He was quite nice.'

'He was quite nice! Is that all? But I saw you enjoyed his company. You amaze me, Hedwig. When I was your age, I knew when I liked a man and when I did not. And when I did, I was not ashamed to say so.'

'And how!'

'Franz, please. Count Szalay is coming on Monday night, Hedwig, as your father told you, and I expect you to try and make a better impression. I want him to feel at home here. He is a stranger and has no friends. And, as you can imagine, he cannot return to his country. I daresay he told you.'

'No.'

'He is too well bred to talk about his misfortunes. But as long as the present regime lasts, he has to stay away. What has the world come to, I sometimes think? Humanity turns against the best and noblest of their own kind. We should thank the Holy Virgin on our knees, Hedwig, that we are safe and happy here.'

'The Hungarian regime won't last long, Melanie. I would not take it too seriously. Although it is no joke for the fellow. Positively no joke.'

'I am glad that we agree,' said the Baroness mildly. 'What did you talk about with him, Hedwig?' and she gave an imperious tap on the back of the settee.

'He told me about his sister. He said I reminded him of her,' replied Hedwig hurriedly, as though pronouncing something which was distasteful to her.

'How charming of him. What a wonderful compliment he paid you. The perfect man of the world,' cried the Baroness.

'What is so charming about it?' asked Baron Kreslov and he looked from his wife to his daughter. 'It may be a damned impudence for all I know. After all, who is the fellow? What is he? Sister here and sister there. He can stick her behind his hat-band, for all I care.'

As an answer to her husband's words the Baroness folded her arms and raised her eyes to the ceiling as though to invoke heaven to be witness to her suffering.

'I merely want to impress on Hedwig that there is nothing wrong in being friendly towards a man from whose friendship she can only benefit. I don't think I am being unreasonable, am I, Franz?'

For a while she looked into space.

The Baron made a noise like a sigh and a grunt.

Hedwig looked obstinately at the tips of her bronze leather shoes.

The Baroness rose. 'I won't say any more. I am the last person to force my opinion on to other people. I can only counsel and advise. But I think Hedwig, that you should know by now that your well-being is very near to my heart. Unfortunately, times have changed. When I was young, there were always plenty of suitable young men about who were only too willing to be attentive.'

'Ah, ah!' said the Baron.

'What do you mean, Franz? Are you insinuating, perhaps, that I had to wait till you came along?'

'Not at all, Melanie.'

'What do you mean then? There was young Karl Libald, for instance, who used to make such pretty poems at every occasion. He was a most devoted admirer of mine.'

'I don't know about pretty. I was never privileged to see them. But as we are already delving into the past, let me remind you that he joined Jaeger & Co., and went bankrupt very prettily a few years later.'

'Is that my fault? Do you have to dig up those incidents as though I were responsible for them?'

'Not at all, Melanie. Nothing is further from my mind.'

'Very well, then. What good does it do, talking about it? This cannot possibly interest Hedwig. As I was saying, Hedwig, times have changed. But there you sit and dream. Your great-grandmother drove out one day with her father when she was fifteen and a stranger saw her passing by in the carriage, found out who she was, went to their house the next day and proposed to her parents. But even in those days this was an exception. Sometimes I believe that this is what you are waiting for.'

'Oh, that old story,' said the Baron. 'I can guarantee you

that they did not welcome him with open arms and made their enquiries first. Stranger – and – and – carriage. Don't bother me with it. And Hedwig does not expect anything from anybody. And why should she? There is positively no reason for it.'

'How right you are, Franz. As always,' said the Baroness kindly. 'I was only trying to bring it home to your daughter how difficult things are – in general.'

'Well, we shan't put the world to rights. Not this evening, in any case. I am going upstairs now. I want to have a last look at the Stock Exchange bulletin.'

Hedwig got up as well. 'I am sorry, Mama,' she murmured and gave her mother a sidelong glance of hatred.

The Baroness looked fondly into her face and kissed her on the forehead.

CHAPTER 15

IT WAS three o'clock in the afternoon. The main part of the sky was blue, but on the horizon stood a long, white cloud, ribbed and crinkled like a strip of sea-sand laid bare by the receding tide. The air was warm and still.

Beneath the tumbled-down roof the flies swarmed round the hayrick, and, from a rusty green tap, water trickled into a battered bucket and overflowed into the earthy grooves formed between the gravel.

Behind the stables, the trees of the Baumgarten stretched as far as the eye could see, and, beyond the entrance which was barred by a crude gate made of unplaned tree trunks, one could perceive a neatly raked sand path which was bordered on both sides by geranium beds and meandering grass walks. On the right stood a small house with ivy clad walls.

Mr. Robinson, the riding master, sat on the steps of the ramshackle palisaded hut which served as office and bridle room. He was peeling an apple with a penknife.

He wore black boots and string-coloured whipcord breeches, an egg-yolk coloured waistcoat, a none too clean white linen coat and a dark green felt hat with a square crown. He was seventy years old and he sat rather gingerly, for his knees were stiff and so was his back. He had the smiling, pink, and honest face and the steady glass clear eyes of an old farmer, but there was such a look of forceful malice about him, that it seemed as though he were only masquerading as a sweet natured old man.

For the last fifteen years the wealthy ladies in Prague had been paying him to be insulted by the hour and to judge by his countenance, he had experienced no difficulty in discharging this service.

Count Szalay jumped over the gate and then helped Hedwig to climb over.

Mr. Robinson kicked the parings of the apple half way across the yard and rose to his feet with some difficulty, but the cheerful smile did not vanish from his face for an instant.

'A good day, Miss Kreslov and the gentleman,' he said with his high-pitched, hoarse voice. 'How is my best girl today? You have gone and been unfaithful to me, as I see. Still, I don't mind, I am used to it. You don't have to tell me what girls are. You are dreadful, you women. So you have got yourself a gentleman friend? High time, too. Life is sweet. It's difficult for you girls. You don't want to be alone all the time and on the other hand you don't want to make yourself cheap. But Miss Kreslov, sir, there you've got something good, something real. Aren't I awful? Always says what I think.' He chuckled with delighted malice.

The Count stuck his eyeglass beneath his raised brow and gave his inward smile, as though he were enjoying a secret joke.

Hedwig blushed and turned her head from side to side.

'Well, sir, how do you feel? You feel fine? You feel like riding? What shall I do about it? Give you a mount?'

The Count gazed at him without moving his face.

'And you can ride, sir?'

'I can.'

'I did not ask you if you could sit on a horse. I asked if you could ride.'

'Mr. Robinson,' said Hedwig imploringly.

'Ah, Miss Kreslov, God bless her heart! Always sweet and kind. The lady speaks up for you, sir. So be it. Which one am I to give you? You are not heavy, let me have a look at you. But you are longer in the leg than I thought at first. The gentleman is very deceitful in his legs, Miss Kreslov, you watch out. If I give Ginger to the lady, he can have Joyful and I will take Spider. Or he can take Spider, if you want to ride out by yourselves. I don't care. I've been in the saddle since six in the morning and I could do with a rest. I caught a cold. Three times I got up last night and went to the wife's bed, but she would not let me do what I wanted, and now I've got a cold. You women! If you want to go alone, I don't mind. The horses will always come back, and what happens to you is your own look-out.'

'I should hate to put you to any inconvenience,' said the Count. 'I think Miss Kreslov can trust herself to me.'

'Just as you say, sir. You won't have any trouble with her. But don't gallop. Any fool can gallop and then the horses get all het up and bolt before you know where you are. A nice, ladylike trot and your horse well collected, that's what I like and no showing off. One is thrown and gets up with a laugh and the other goes down and has a cracked shoulder. I don't want you to fall. The ground is as hard as a stone, we have had no rain for a week. But head up and the world belongs to you. Life is sweet.'

With this Mr. Robinson went to the gate, shouted a few words, and almost at once a stable boy appeared who received orders to harness Ginger and Spider.

'Spider is nice and smooth,' said Mr. Robinson. 'But he is light in the mouth, so you be careful.'

'I shall find out soon enough,' replied the Count.

'I am telling you, so that you don't have to find out. That's what I am here for. Don't mind me, sir, always says what I think. When you come to my age – I am seventy-five – you don't bother with being polite.'

They watched Ginger who was being led out, a sedate roan cob with a nasty rolling eye.

'You don't know the park, do you, sir? It's not a bad place, you will see. But nothing like Hyde Park. I used to go there when I was young. A little beauty she was too, black as the devil. In those days that was all we had, we poor folk. Hotel rooms cost eight and six, that was for the toffs, we couldn't afford it.' He then proceded to give further details concerning the amorous habits of the English upper classes as compared to those of the people and, counting the time elapsed between his youth and the present day, he confessed his age to be sixty-five, seventy, and seventy-five, as the mood took him.

At last both horses were got ready. Mr. Robinson professed his scorn for the mounting block and the Count gave Hedwig a leg up.

The stable boy was ordered to bring a cane for Miss Kreslov.

'I shall want one, too,' said the Count.

'You don't want the stick to Spider. He's got enough spirit as it is and to spare. You don't want to break his heart, do you? You break Miss Kreslov's heart, that's better.' And Mr. Robinson gave his malicious chuckle.

'I insist,' said the Count. 'I don't feel dressed without it.'

'Have your way. A crop for the gentleman. And see that you don't lose it. But you don't want to have those spurs. Take them off, sir, you don't know the horse, let me tell you. He don't take to them kindly. He's got his own ideas.'

'So have I.'

Mr. Robinson and the stable boy, who had now returned from the bridle room with a riding crop, stood and looked at the Count's beautiful boots. He wore large silver spurs, the wheels of which were made of old silver coins from which time and usage had rubbed off nearly all the marking.

'Hem!' said Mr. Robinson and his eyes slid up and down those boots with an expression as though to say: 'Can you take the responsibility of that, my boy? Are you sure you can?' His mouth was pulled to one side as though he had swallowed a burning morsel. 'You'll have to do damn well to get away with this,' said his glance, and he took the crop from the boy and flicked with its thong over the offending spurs.

'Well, good luck,' he said at last. 'Trot them slowly to let them warm up. And Miss Kreslov, remember your wrists, don't work them up and down like a washerwoman. And tuck in your behind, sit on it, don't show it. And straighten up on top, show what you've got there. My God! if I was a woman, I would be proud of it. And don't lean forward when you canter, the horse wants to get there first, not you. Aren't I awful?'

The Count had mounted, meanwhile, and adjusted his stirrups, while Mr. Robinson, turning his back to him, held Ginger's head and gave directions to the stable boy in order to get the straps even, while he kept up a steady flow of embarrassing details about Hedwig's anatomy.

There was a snort and a clatter of hooves. Ginger reared for an instant as the Count cantered in two strides to the gate, cleared it in a high jump, cantered a few paces on the narrow sand path and wheeled his horse round in a turn with not an inch to spare, took the gate again and finally brought his horse to a standstill close to Hedwig. He patted the animal's head.

'Are you ready, Miss Kreslov?' he asked with one eyebrow raised above the monocle and pointed with his crop to the gate.

The stable boy opened it without a word.

'Shall I take the lead slowly till we are out in the open? And then, I hope, you will be good enough to tell me which is your favourite way.'

'Good-bye, Mr. Robinson,' cried Hedwig and raised her cane with an apologetic smile.

They went out at a slow walk.

The riding master sat down on the steps, pushed his hat back and picked up the apple from the window sill, where he had placed it.

'Pepi,' he said. 'Have you ever seen anything like it? There's nothing to jumping, any fool can jump. But the way he wheels round on that space outside, in full canter and no more room for turning than the palm of my hand. I did not think it could be done. It isn't decent to ride as well as that. Mark my word, he is no gentleman. Feed my apple to the horses. I've lost my appetite.'

131

Once past the small house, they turned into a pebble-paved road, walled off on one side by a row of high planks. Mounds of coarse sand and crusted lime were set against this fence, piles of broken bricks and crumbled stones, and two dead tree trunks exposed their knotted roots as though frozen in black agony.

Between this accumulation of decay grew a mass of nettles which, with their sharply jagged leaves, formed a continuation to the ragged and angular outlines of the rubble. It smelt of dust and mortar.

'There is a building site behind the paling,' said Hedwig. 'Someone started to work on it two years ago. Afterwards it was abandoned again. It is not very pleasant to look at, but in a minute we shall be out of it. Unfortunately, there is no other way from the stables to the park.'

'Back stage effect,' said the Count. 'Have you ever been behind the wings, Miss Kreslov? It is a similar impression, the drabness which one should never see.'

'I can imagine it. But I don't know it,' replied Hedwig. 'I suppose it is drab, as you say. But very interesting at the same time, isn't it?'

'My God, how am I to answer, Miss Kreslov? If I tell you it is fascinating, you will be envious and feel more shy and isolated than you already are; and if I say that it is dirty and dusty and repellent, you will think that I am a prig. I'll try and compromise. In my opinion, there is a thrill in it for certain natures. Schoolboys of all ages glory in it, I should say. Some people like to fish in troubled waters. Dogs like to roll in filth. It is that sort of attraction. Does that mean anything to you?'

'I don't know.'

'But you would like to try it out for yourself?'

'We'll take the way to the left now,' said Hedwig breath-lessly. She felt his eyes on her and turned her head away. They entered into a pleached avenue. The trees had been struck by frost in the winter and were not in leaf, but the bare boughs were so closely interlaced that they barred the sun and wind. Looking up, the riders could see the blue sky as though through the meshes of a black net. But again and again they were forced to bend their heads to avoid the low-hanging branches and breathed the dank air laden with the smell of rotting leaves which rose from the ground.

There are places which have a climate and a season of their own; in the avenue, beneath the barren and entwined roof, it was forever winter.

Hedwig tightened her reins. 'Shall we have a canter now?' she asked. 'Afterwards, when we are out in the open, we shall have to go slowly for a while, till we are past the restaurant.'

'Canter? What next? You are dreadful, you women,' said the Count with the intonation of the riding master. 'And pull your hat well down, Miss Kreslov, to shield your pretty eyes. Aren't I awful? Always says what I think.'

Hedwig blushed and adjusted her round black hat and looked up to him as though asking for approval.

'You look a proper treat. Fit to be seen in Hyde Park,' exclaimed the Count, still imitating Mr. Robinson's voice.

Laughing, they sped over the rutted path through the brown twilight, screened on all sides from sight and sound. The Count kept a head's length in front of Hedwig. A sense of shyness prevented her from looking straight at him, but glancing ahead of her, with her chin held high as she had been taught, she could see his hands in the yellow leather gloves resting firmly on the bridle, with the reins streaming in two arched lines from between his fingers.

Tree after tree rushed past her, woven into an intricate pattern of twisted knots, shadowy and monotonous.

The Count's horse was dappled, it looked as though small grey apples had been painted on to the skin which was as white as porcelain. In the dimness it seemed like a phantom beast, formed by the play of light and shade. Rising and falling in the saddle with dreamy slowness, she was only aware that the curved lines of the animal's neck, breast, and shoulders ran into his hands and were held by them. She was happy.

Suddenly she perceived the bright green parkscape standing in the blue air, framed by the last skeleton branches of the avenue.

The Count turned round and stretched out his arm, to make sure that her horse would slow down. Spider stumbled and tossed his head. The twilight dissolved into sunshine. The soft path changed into gravel and the thudding sound of the cantering hooves changed into the brisk and crunching noise of trotting. The shriek and laughter of children came shrilly from the distance. They were out in the open.

The Count reined in his horse and fell back to Hedwig's side.

'Nice?' he asked.

'Very nice.'

They slowed down to a walk.

'You are not missing Mr. Robinson?'

'Of course not. I felt so happy during our canter. I suppose because he was not there. It was so nice of you to take

134

the lead. He generally keeps at the back and whips up my horse unexpectedly from behind and makes it rear.'

'They are all the same. I was taught once by a Cavalry sergeant and when we were in the *manège* he used to fasten a piece of string across the path to unseat us. It was his greatest pleasure. The only way with these people is to freeze them. Mud is bound by frost.'

'Yes,' she said thoughtfully. 'And you like Spider?'

'He is not bad. He tried a few tricks at first and then he wanted to go to sleep on me but we came to an understanding.'

'I imagine that you are used to wonderful horses,' said Hedwig.

'I have been, Miss Kreslov. They had many virtues, but all of them have committed an unpardonable mistake. They died.'

'Oh,' said Hedwig and looked at him, not sure whether to smile or be grave. Her fresh pink lips were half parted and her face beneath the stiff black hat was soft and eager.

'You may well say oh,' replied the Count cheerfully, and they both laughed as though he had said something very funny.

'Horses altogether are a melancholy subject,' he continued. 'I lost a few thousand the other day on the turf.'

'I am terribly sorry,' and Hedwig turned her eyes to him, full with pity.

He raised an eyebrow. 'It does not matter,' he said, 'it was not my money in any case.'

'Oh!' said Hedwig. She glanced straight ahead of her between Ginger's ears. The Count watched her with a calculating expression.

'And while we are on the subject of betting, Miss Kreslov, I would be very tempted to put up a little wager. Arrange a little contest. Not with horses but between our elders and betters. A battle of wills, so to speak. What would you say – your mother hardly knows Mr. Robinson, does she?'

'She only saw him once or twice.'

'Just as I thought. What would you say then, if we arranged a meeting? Who would emerge with flying colours? I take it that you, as a dutiful daughter, would place your money on Mama.'

'Count Szalay,' she murmured with a shocked voice. Her face coloured with pleasure and she contemplated her mount's neck with a delighted smile.

The gravel walk twisted yellow, neat, and glossy between weeping willows, maples, and copper beeches, and between their trunks shimmered the cloudy green of the more distant trees. The park seemed to be deserted. In front of the riders a crescent of shrubbery hid the view; but every step brought them nearer to the sound of voices.

'In a minute we shall be at the restaurant,' said Hedwig. 'It is always quite full when the weather is nice. It is very popular, you know. We are never allowed to go there but once Ali's horse bolted and she went in and had a lemonade. She said she needed it after the fright, so nobody could——'

Her horse gave an angry snort, got up into the air and tried to turn sideways, while Spider put his head in front of Ginger's forelegs, as though he wanted to bar the other's way and be off in the opposite direction. It looked as though it was going to be one of those really good mix-ups for which horses are peculiarly gifted.

'Allow me,' said the Count. He leaned forward, reached

with his whip hand across to Hedwig and took hold of Ginger's reins. He dragged the horse backwards and at the same time straightened Spider's head and brought him to a standstill.

'That did it,' he said and pointed with his riding crop to the ground. At the foot of the shrubbery lay a crumpled piece of newspaper.

'I slipped my stirrups,' said Hedwig. 'Just a second.'

'Take your time. I'll hold your animal.'

He gathered the reins of both horses in his left hand and put his right arm round her shoulder to steady her. For a moment she leant against him and he held her a bit closer. Then she sat up straight.

'It is all right now,' she said. 'Thank you very much.'

He moved his arm from her shoulder slowly, as though with reluctance. 'Ready, Miss Kreslov? I will keep your reins for another minute till we are past the offending object.'

They set off. The horses walked sedately and sheepishly past the dark-leaved bushes.

'I shall restore your freedom now, Miss Kreslov. I always believe in letting charming young women have their way. Unfortunately, I cannot keep you on the lead for ever.'

'I am sorry I gave you all this trouble, Count Szalay. Ginger can be a nuisance. But, of course, it is my fault. I should have kept him on a tighter rein.'

'Not at all. You can thank your excellent Mr. Robinson for having slipped your stirrups. I noticed already when you were mounted that he had put them up too short and it does not give you a chance to use your knees. I did not say anything, of course, I did not want to be meddlesome. But will you let me adjust them for you in the future? I should love to meddle. Ah! and there is the place where your sister defied her expensive upbringing. We must come here one day. Better late than never, don't you think, Miss Kreslov? And to judge from the little I know about you, I think that you will have to drink at least a thousand lemonades to make up for outstanding arrears.'

On the left of the walk stood the restaurant. It was a long and low building of sand coloured stone, fronted by a glassed-in veranda which was framed with a white-painted border of wooden fretwork. A few steps led to a vast square laid with raw planks, set with four rows of tables, which were covered with red and white checked cloths and surrounded by green iron seats. The veranda looked empty, but the open air café was filled with grown-ups and children, drinking coffee, milk, and poisonously red and green sparkling waters and eating bread and butter, cheese tarts, and yeast cake filled with sliced plums and poppy seed.

On the opposite side was a lawn and round flowerbeds planted with forget-me-nots and red tulips, all of exactly the same height and shape, where several women chased after runaway offspring, while others led their howling captives back to the tables. The air resounded with clinking and clatter, cries of distress, scolding and laughter. Two waiters in stained white coats swam among the clamorous crowd with their laden trays held high above their shoulders as though carrying a precious burden which had to be kept away from any soiling contact.

On the far end of the lawn stood a park attendant with a large white moustache and a blue uniform. Above his crossed arms he contemplated the scene with an air of detachment and responsibility like a keeper of caged animals who is used to the antics of his charges.

Hedwig and the Count did not ride past the restaurant, but took a way which led in a semicircle behind the flower-beds. From there they gained a riding path which stretched between rows of chestnuts. On their right in the distance, they saw a rose parterre, a dilapidated greenhouse and a string of empty iron benches, flashing in the sun. They trotted briskly through the silent green till they came to a clearing. They stopped.

'In which direction would you like to go now?' asked Hedwig. 'The bridle path continues round there and into the park. Or we could cut through the wood beyond the open space. It is very pretty, but bumpy and full of holes.'

'Which way do you think would suit me better, Miss Kreslov?'

'The bumpy one. The park is too tame for you.'

'Is that so?' said the Count with that mixture of amuse-ment and displeasure which one shows in the company of a precocious child. 'And why, if I may ask?'

'I just thought,' murmured Hedwig.

'You thought quite right, Miss Kreslov. I have been talk-ing carelessly and you concluded very accurately that I am a bit – well, the less said about me, the better. I must be more on my guard in future. From now on I shall talk about nothing but the scenery.'

'No, please don't!' cried Hedwig vehemently. She even leaned towards him and caught his sleeve.

'What? No scenery?' asked the Count with well-feigned surprise.

'No, please.'

139

'What shall it be, then?'

'The way you gamble. And how people give you money. And – and everything. And what it is like – no, I'll ask you another time.'

'At last you have come to life. You are charming, Miss Kreslov.' He took her hand.

She looked away. 'Shall we go through the wood? I think you will find it very pretty and picturesque.'

He glanced at her with pretended despair. 'I tell you that you are charming and you answer that the wood is picturesque. Well-brought-up young girls are very bewildering. I am not used to them.'

'You aren't?' she asked eagerly.

'Certainly not.' He raised her fingers, drew the glove away and kissed her wrist. Then he placed her hand on the saddle. 'You lead,' he said.

They skirted the clearing. A small stone bridge spanned a ravine full of stones, twigs and bracken. Brambles, elders and hazelnuts rustled against the horses' flanks and parted and closed with a hissing sound like tearing silk. Stripling oaks grew among grassy boulders, and above the thorny, sombre and untidy undergrowth, the checkered stems of birch trees rose thin, clean, and smooth against the delicate blue sky.

'There are lots of mushrooms here in summer,' remarked Hedwig.

'And you are not allowed to pick them because they might be poisonous. You don't have to tell me,' replied the Count. 'The Baroness would implore Heaven to witness your foolhardiness and your Father would say that there is positively no reason to run the risk, is there? As you see,

Miss Kreslov, I have not eaten two dinners in your house for nothing.'

Hedwig giggled.

'Shall we dismount for a while, Miss Krelsov? And give the horses a breather? I feel very friendly and mellow – strictly towards the horses, of course.'

Without waiting for her assent, he jumped down and tethered Spider to a tree.

'You had better stay in the saddle till I tie up my horse. He is not quite himself after our fright.'

A minute later he came up to Hedwig to help her down. She dropped into his arms like a ripe plum. Other men would have been too slow or too impetuous. But the Count took her hat off and kissed her with the cool elegance which was peculiar to all his movements. Then he made her sit down and gave her a cigarette. Her hand trembled as she held it towards the flame of his lighter. He put an arm on her shoulder and stroked her hair and the nape of her neck, watching her attentively, while they smoked in silence.

At last he said: 'I won't apologize. It serves you right. My brother officers used to say on such occasions: "Good God, I don't know what came over me and you are such a nice girl, too." '

She turned to him with a smile. 'Did they?'

'Of course. That would have gone down well with the scenery. But you would not let me follow that line. Don't you regret it now? I can still say something of the sort if you wish it.'

'No,' said Hedwig.

'You amaze me, Miss Kreslov. Am I to understand that you do not curse the day when you first set eyes on me?'

141

She shook her head.

'I am utterly bewildered,' said the Count. 'I wish I had more experience.'

He took her cigarette and threw it away. She fell into his arms. A few minutes later he gave her a last kiss on the forehead and rose to his feet.

'Cigarette? This is the point where one says: I can't stand this any more. Good God, do you think I am made of iron?'

'Really?' said Hedwig with great interest.

'Of course. But with ladies of a different class one does not ask that question. As they have not been brought up as well as you, they know all the answers.'

He helped her to get up and collected her hat, gloves and cane from the ground.

'You put me in such a difficult position, Miss Kreslov. I am used to making proposals to pretty young women, but not honourable ones. And yet – you know – I cannot bear to see you going on the way you are. I don't want to see you any more standing about at receptions and being anxious to say the right thing. I think we understand each other. Will you marry me?'

'Yes,' said Hedwig. 'But Mama?'

'Leave her to me. Haven't I courted her enough already? I will appear tomorrow and pay my addresses to her. She will give her blessing without a murmur. And believe me, even if I told her that I want to take you to that vulgar restaurant, she would be delighted. Shall I do it?'

'You can't!' said Hedwig.

'Of course I can. I will tell her tomorrow, when she overflows with maternal feelings.'

'No, please don't. It is too worrying for jokes.'

CHAPTER 16

BENEATH THE wreathed ormolu dome of the small
Empire clock, the two feathered arrows of bronze pointed
to half past eleven. The pendulum, cast in the shape of a
bee, swung ceaselessly between the two black pillars which
supported the structure, with the vigorous and yet melancholy insistence which is part of the Napoleonic splendour.

'They take such a long time,' said Hedwig. She frowned
and lowered her eyelids, partly because she was unstrung
and partly because the morning sun struck blinding flashes
from the lead-rimmed squares of the Empire mirror, while
the floor was showered with dazzling spots, reflections
of the eagles which spread their bronze wings over the
square head of the bed.

'He's hardly been five minutes,' replied Fräulein Lotte
from the window seat, where she was engaged in pulling up
with a fine steel hook the dropped mesh of a silk stocking.

'Not even five minutes,' she continued, without looking
up from her work. 'And it will take a good time yet. You
can't expect him to come blundering into the drawing-room
like an ox in the field and blurt it all out in a minute? He's
got to make conversation first.'

'If it takes much longer, it will mean that Mama is making

objections.' Hedwig closed her eyes for a second and touched her brow with her hand. Her face was white and her lips pale. Beneath her eyes lay brownish shadows.

'Dear me, why should she be making objections? She is quite gone on him herself. You have only got to look, the way she talks to him. Now don't fret yourself, Hedy. Keep your hair nice and your stockings straight and God will see to the rest!'

'Do I look all right, Fräulein Lotte?'

'As nice as anybody could wish for.' The housekeeper raised her eyes and the black earrings dangled round her faithful face, as though to emphasize her opinion.

'I think we could put a spot of red on the lips,' she added. 'It does not matter if you are pale in the face, that's as it should be, you don't want to look like a peasant girl with red cheeks, but you could do with some colour just the same. Mama has not forbidden it and what is not forbidden is allowed.'

'We have got a lipstick hidden behind Ali's stamp album,' said Hedwig. 'She got it from Gerty Lavacek. They put it on in the lavatory in school – you know.'

'In between being sick from smoking cigarettes and worse,' said Fräulein Lotte. 'You can't teach me anything about young girls. Now fetch it quick and don't use it straight, put it on with your little finger. That makes it look more natural.'

After a while Hedwig returned looking happy and very pretty. Her lips were faintly rouged.

'I am glad I did it, Fräulein. I don't care now about anything any more. If Mama notices it, let her. Shall I put my pearls on?'

'You might just as well,' replied Fräulein Lotte. 'You won't be wearing them much longer – take my word for it. In a while you will be having pearls as large as cherries, you can trust your father for that. And it's quite as it should be. You will need good pearls.' She said this with a quiet, matter-of-course pride, as though she herself were used to the most expensive jewellery.

Hedwig put on her necklace and lingered in front of the mirror, looking at herself with a rather severe expression by which she tried to hide her excitement. She wore a dark blue wool dress with a small white embroidered collar and cuffs.

'Now you just sit down and look into the garden. Green is a relaxing colour,' remarked Fräulein Lotte. 'When I went to the eye specialist last time, you need no glasses, he said, just walk a lot among the grass and the trees and look at it as much as you can, it will rest you.'

'Yes, yes,' said Hedwig.

Fräulein Lotte's wisdom was the latest acquisition in her rich store of homely remedies. All of them were eminently well suited for a person dealing with pampered and highly strung children: they were completely ineffective and yet bore the dignity of a real medicine or medical ritual.

'Just sit down,' continued Fräulein Lotte. 'And make your body all limp. When your muscles are relaxed, your mind relaxes, too.'

There was a knock on the door and the footman entered. Neither Hedwig nor the housekeeper looked up.

'The Baroness says will Miss Kreslov please come down. They are in the small drawing-room.'

'Miss Hedwig will be down in a minute,' replied Fräulein Lotte.

When they were alone, Hedwig remained on the spot and said: 'I don't feel at all excited now. I hope Mama won't weep or do anything *génant*.'

'Dear me. As though she were in the habit of it. Run along now.'

It seemed as though Hedwig was not in a hurry to leave. She took a last long glance in the mirror. Then she walked slowly to the door.

'Fräulein Lotte,' she said with her hand on the door knob, 'what if he has to kiss me in front of Mama?'

'Good gracious, nobody will expect him to kiss you, he is a gentleman first and last. Off you go, Hedy. You have got nothing to worry about. Whatever he does, he will do the right thing, he is an aristocrat to his fingertips. And so he should be. You can't be expected to marry just anybody who comes along.'

The Baroness Kreslov and Count Szalay sat opposite each other on cherry-coloured satin chairs in the smallest of the suite of drawing-rooms. On the lace-clothed table between them stood an open *bonbonnière* of dark blue porcelain with a border of golden lozenges and there were screwed-up scraps of silver paper on an ashtray in front of the Baroness, which betrayed that she was somewhat excited. Usually, she smoothed out the wrapping paper of the chocolates she had eaten.

The Count's hat, with his gloves tucked inside it, reposed on the floor by his feet.

A decanter filled with sherry, and two untouched glasses, were placed on an oval silver tray on the top of the harpsichord.

The Baroness wore a small-checked chestnut-brown

tweed suit and a white silk blouse, at the neck of which she had pinned her diamond hoop, but unfortunately not quite in the centre, so that one wing of the collar was pulled downwards. Her grey hair stood full and slightly untidy round her fresh-coloured face. She held a lace-bordered handkerchief between her fingers.

'My dear Count Szalay, I am very much surprised. Very pleasantly surprised, you will allow me to say so. You have not had much time to get to know each other, but then, you are not a schoolboy, you are a man of the world and you must know your own heart.'

She laid her head to one side and looked at him with mild determination.

The Count crossed one leg over the other and played with his eyeglass. 'You have taken the words out of my mouth, madam.'

'Of course you understand that I cannot give you a definite answer. My husband will want to have a talk with you.'

The Count inclined his head.

'But as far as I am concerned, my dear Count, I must say that I am deeply moved. I am convinced that you will make Hedwig very happy. That is all that counts with me.'

'You are very kind. I don't know if I deserve it. Yet somehow I was hoping – you have great understanding, dear Baroness. This is the reason why I came to you straight away. I knew you would look beyond conventions and forgive my apparent haste.'

'My dear Count, as though there was anything to forgive. On the contrary, I am gratified that you came to me first. If only others had done the same in similar circumstances!'

She raised her eyes to the ceiling. 'I often wish my judgment had been wrong, for the sake of others.'

'So I may put myself into your hands?'

'You may, indeed. And here comes my little girl. I don't know what to say, Hedwig. The Count will say it no doubt much better than I could.'

They both rose. Hedwig looked at her mother.

'Is Fräulein Lotte upstairs?' asked the Baroness in a matter-of-fact tone of voice.

'Yes, Mama.'

'I have to speak to her for five minutes. You will excuse me. And offer the Count a glass of sherry, my dear. No, nothing for me. Perhaps afterwards.'

She raised her head and gave her daughter a commanding glance of her bulging blue eyes, similar to the one which meant 'keep your shoulders back', but holding a deeper significance.

The Baroness was true to her word. Exactly five minutes later she reappeared in the drawing-room. The Count and Hedwig were leaning against the harpsichord and sipping sherry.

The Count took a few steps towards her, one eyebrow raised and smiling as though he were enjoying a secret joke.

'This is a very happy day for me, dear Baroness.'

She extended one hand which he kissed, and reached with the other to her daughter.

'This is wonderful!' she said, gazing fondly at both. Hedwig gave an embarrassed smile and looked into space above her mother's head.

They sat down. The footman brought another glass and the Baroness drank her sherry. In between, she raised her handkerchief and dabbed her perfectly dry eyes.

'Not another word,' she said. 'We must wait till my husband comes home. I daresay that you are very surprised Hedwig, but I am not. That is why you see me so calm. I knew it all along, only I did not say anything, because I did not want to interfere. I know my daughter much better than she does herself, my dear Count. I would not be a good mother if it were otherwise.'

She added a few more observations of a similar nature which she pronounced with great dignity but not much conviction.

The Count received her words with well-feigned interest and inclined his head from time to time with an appraising air as though he were saying, 'Well done. Continue.' Hedwig looked at the tips of her shoes and twisted the pearls round her throat.

A few minutes later, the Count left, after accepting an invitation for dinner for the evening. The Baroness's last words were most cordial although a trifle absent-minded. And while she assured him again that the final decision rested with her husband, her brain was already preoccupied with the question whether Schenck & Weimann would make a price reduction if she ordered the Irish linen for the trousseau in bales and unbleached.

CHAPTER 17

IT WAS the first meal *en famille* at which the Count took part. All the leaves had been taken out of the dining-table and now it looked absurdly small and isolated beneath the vast coffered ceiling. This isolation was enhanced by the candlelight which drew its narrow circles on the cloth. The walls seemed far away. On either side of the tapestries burned the sconces behind little parchment shields. Their watery light streamed over the fairytale woods and showed them blue and green, deep and remote, like distant land-scapes seen through a window from a dark room.

As usual, the Baroness had taken no special trouble over her dress but had been generous with her jewels. Like many rich women, she believed that precious stones are not worn for their appearance but because they are the symbols of wealth and as such can be relied upon to be more impressive than the prettiest dress. She wore an old claret-coloured chiffon gown with unfashionably long sleeves. A collar of diamonds and rubies enclosed her long and robust neck and two ruby brooches fastened the strip of lace which partly concealed thec oarse-grained skin above her breast.

On her right were the Count and Hedwig. On her left

Fräulein Lotte and Alexandrine. The Baron sat opposite his wife at the foot of the table. He looked tired. While the others sat upright and without touching the oval, caned backs of the walnut chairs, he alone sat as he pleased, with one elbow on the table and his shoulders hunched forward, so that the stiff shirt of his dinner suit protruded in an unsightly bulge. He and the Count seemed to be the only ones who were completely at their ease.

The Count was so smoothly groomed and well brushed that this seemed to have been achieved effortlessly and therefore looked as though it were his natural state. He wore pearls instead of buttons to fasten his dress-shirt, which was of soft *piqué* with a raised beehive pattern. Both were unusual; in fact, they had never been seen in Prague before. He knew that he was the centre of attention at the table and it was obvious that he enjoyed it.

Hedwig at his side never exchanged a look with him and ate very little. Her hair, dark red in the candlelight, lay in rigid waves about her face and enhanced her severe and marble white beauty. Her dress was of the same pale blue silk as that of her sister but of a more grown-up cut.

Alexandrine had a sulky and attentive expression. She resented being dressed in the same style as Hedwig, especially as she was convinced that her own fair hair was superior to that of her sister and that the blue dress had been chosen for her sister's and not for her advantage. She resented the fact that she had been riding in the afternoon with Mr. Robinson, while Hedwig had gone off with their visitor to a different part of the Baumgarten. She resented that she would be sent upstairs after the coffee. She took her food fitfully, often laying knife and fork aside, listening, trying to divine the mysteries which she felt to be hidden beneath the small talk of the adults.

Fräulein Lotte took small, mincing mouthfuls and chewed slowly, which she considered polite. Proud in her knowledge that she was part of the company, she was thinking with satisfaction of Mademoiselle Bergot's solitary meal in the schoolroom. The Frenchwoman was always excluded from evening meals. Baron Kreslov said that he could not stand the sight of her rabbit teeth more than once a day.

The Baron ate his dry rice and chopped meat hastily, and with occasional grunts. The others were served with mushroom omelette, grilled pike with a sour egg-sauce, hot ham with spinach and Madeira sauce, chestnut pudding with cream, and Gruyère cheese with red pepper fried on triangles of white bread.

At last the meal was over. The Baroness rose. She gave an imperious glance to Alexandrine who was starting to suck a slice of lemon which she had fished out from her finger bowl. She was at the age when a perverse appetite for unripe fruit and acid foods is common.

Another look, kinder but bracing, went to Hedwig, who straightened her back.

'Please stay,' said the Baroness to the men who had also risen. 'I hope that you will not join us until you have finished your cigars. This does not mean that I dislike cigars as a rule, my dear Count. But my throat is a bit sensitive just now. At the end of a party the other night, my voice was completely finished.'

As soon as they were alone, the Baron pushed his chair aside. 'If Melanie thinks that I am going to sit here, she is mistaken. Cigars – all very well. But there is positively no reason why we should not have softer chairs, is there?'

They went into the adjoining room and sat down on two leather armchairs, in a corner formed by a bookcase and a black marble pedestal bearing a philosopher's bust. The footman brought a burning candle, while the Baron produced a cigar box.

The Count declined and lit a cigarette.

'Well, then,' said his host. 'Melanie told me. Hedwig told me. Fräulein Lotte told me. I suppose tomorrow I shall hear it on the Stock Exchange. I tell you straight out, I shan't put any obstacles in your way. But I want to know where I stand. You seem very nice, yes, you do. I can understand Hedwig, I've got eyes in my head. So far so good. But how are your finances, Count Szalay?'

Above the glowing tip of his cigar his eyes, tired and disillusioned, rested on the Count's shirt front.

The Count put his cigarette down and drew himself up.

'Dear sir, I can give you my word of honour as an officer and gentleman, that if I had a lot of money, I should be a rich man.'

The Baron groaned with laughter and fanned himself with his cigar.

'That's all right, my boy. For that alone you deserve her.' He continued in his comfortable, rumbling, tone of voice: 'Any debts? Come clean with me. I know we've got to pay for our luxuries.'

'Clean slate,' said the Count quickly.

'That's something. That's more than I expected.'

For a while they smoked in silence.

'That's settled then,' began the Baron and folded his hands above his watch chain. 'Have the engagement announced in, say, a fortnight and get married in six weeks. That's the best I can do for you. How is that for a bargain?'

'Splendid.'

'I'll tell you how it is. They all want it, so it's no use dragging it out. On the other hand, it's no use my playing for time. I can't make any proper enquiries, all business connections have gone to the dogs in your country, so what's the good? I know who you are and what you are. I suppose sooner or later you will try to get your estates back?'

'I don't think so Baron. I have no experience in farming. I was not brought up to it.'

'All the better. At least I know where I am. What do you say if I put you on one or two boards of directors? At a salary, strictly speaking. I've got to see how you shape first. Three hundred thousand crowns a year. If you don't take to it, we'll find something else for you. I don't expect you to blossom into a miracle man overnight. There is positively no reason why you should. If you get on well, then I'll put you on your feet properly. I am going to open two new factories in Silesia. If that interests you, you can run them. But we shall have to see first.'

The Count nodded thoughtfully.

'Hedwig is a sweet girl,' continued the Baron. 'Once you get her away from Melanie, she will be a changed woman. I can't do anything for her really. It is a shame, but what can I do? You have seen it for yourself how it is.'

'I certainly have,' said the Count.

His host got up and fetched brandy and glasses.

'You can have a liqueur if you like, my boy, anything up and down the menu, all that's good and expensive. I personally can't stand these fancy stuffs.'

'Brandy for me, please.'

'Right. As I was saying. It is a shame. Don't think that I don't know it. Sometimes I sit and worry about the girls. I don't always think about business, you know. I am quite decent. Sometimes I wake up at five in the morning and worry about myself because I am so decent. But what do I do about it? Nothing. Nothing at all.'

He took a gulp of brandy, pushed his chair forward and laid a hand on the Count's arm. 'You are all right. I will make a confession to you. Even if you were not all right, I would have said yes and amen, marry her and be done with it. And do you know why? Because I am a coward. Melanie wants this, that, and the other, and I let her have it. I want my peace and quiet. I am too tired. I can't any more.'

'I'll tell you something,' said the Count.

'Ah, ah, you'll tell me something. Go right ahead my boy,'

'You have heard about Jan Hus?'

'Yes, yes,' replied the Baron suspiciously.

'As you know, he went around shouting his head off about God and truth and was such an embarrassment and so uncomfortable that they had to burn him in the end to shut him up.'

'Yes. On Lake Constance. In fourteen hundred fifteen. We had it at school.'

'Exactly. But at the same time there was Peter Chelcicky who lived in the South of Bohemia and minded his own business.'

'Ah, there,' said the Baron, brightening up, 'that's where they have the big carp ponds. Queer fish, the carp, I have always felt it. I hope he did not eat them. They are no good to anybody.'

'Perhaps he did,' replied the Count cautiously. 'He also wrote a book called "The Net of Faith". And in it he put down that one should not fight evil, even if one was convinced that one knew the real truth and the real good. If you fight evil, you increase evil. I always had a foible for that man. And really, dear Baron, after what you have told me, I do not think that you are a coward. You are a very wise man. Don't fight. It is not worth it.'

'That's good. That's quite true, of course. You are a capital fellow, Count Szalay. I think you and I are going to do well together. I suppose we had better be on the move now. Champagne if you like. Personally, I can't stand it. If you had a stomach as weak as mine, you'd understand.'

Later in the evening, the Baron said to his wife: 'Very clever man, the Count. Unusual though. Like cream. Don't know if I should eat him or drink him.'

'He is extremely charming, Franz.'

'So he is. He could charm the birds off the trees.'

CHAPTER 18

THE PREMATURELY hot weather continued as April changed into May.

The Moldau was at low level. The statue of Roland, with the lion at his feet "rose higher than usual out of the water" and the pedestal, girdled by a green and slimy ring, showed how much the river had receded. Above the round and curly head of the statue, with its smile which had become blurred and imbecile through the passage of hundreds of years, stood the archway which led, between the bridge towers, to the Kleinseite. The air lay stale and dusty over the labyrinthine pattern of the massed houses. The Castle Hill was striped with blue and green, already faded, where lilac and foliage fell over old ramparts and rooftops.

Mr. Maly, walking along the cobbled street, paused several times to wipe his face and change the spray of flowers in its sheath of tissue paper from one hand to the other. He had been asked to tea for five o'clock; it was barely past the hour. But, despite the heat, he walked hurriedly, harrowed by the provincial's fear to be 'missing something which was going on'.

When he was shown into the sunny and flower scented drawing-room in Steffanie Smejkal's flat, he found old

157

Professor Surovy standing by the window, with a coloured glass goblet held high in his hand and tilting his head upwards so that his short white beard pointed towards it.

Steffanie Smejkal, with her hand on Hedwig's arm, stood behind him with their backs turned to the door, while Count Szalay was leaning against the tall walnut frame of the pier glass. In the old mirror the reflection of his fair head was slightly lengthened and tinged with green.

'I have the honour,' said Mr. Maly and showed his pretty white teeth in an angelic smile.

Professor Surovy lowered his arm, dropped his somewhat prophetic attitude and assumed an air of urbanity. Steffanie turned round and stretched out her hand. Mr. Maly pressed the flowers into it.

'How pretty,' she said, without looking inside the wrapping, and laid them aside on a small table. 'Hedwig, this is Mr. Maly,' she added.

'We have met,' replied Mr. Maly.

'I believe so,' said Hedwig.

'And Professor Surovy. And Count Szalay.'

Mr. Maly shook hands vigorously and enthusiastically with both of them.

'Please go on Professor,' said Steffanie.

He resumed his previous posture. 'It is just an old Bohemian glass, dear madam. And red, of course. But not the genuine ruby glass. The old ruby colour was mixed with gold and cannot be reproduced any more.'

'You mean they took their secret with them to their graves?' asked Mr. Maly.

'If you wish to put it that way,' replied the old man with a pained face.

'But how old is it? Eighteenth century?'

'Nothing like it, dear madam. As you see it has a picture cut on it, a landscape with a building. It was meant to be a souvenir – there is always something vulgar about souvenirs. The whole conception is a trifle vulgar. Eighteen hundred and seventy I should say, or even later. The bad taste of the Francis-Joseph period. The old tradition is still there, of course, but very much dimmed unfortunately. We must work away from this trend.'

'You are quite right, Professor,' said Mr. Maly, 'I have always felt it myself. We must work away from this trend. But why really?'

The Professor without glancing in the other's direction, gave the goblet a last twist and placed it on the window sill.

'I don't care,' said Steffanie Smejkal. 'I shall use it for flowers.'

'You should never do that, dear madam. The glass was not meant for that purpose.'

Mr. Maly, getting bored, edged nearer to the Count.

'I thought I saw you the other day at Baroness Kreslov's "at home". You were there, weren't you?'

The Count nodded.

'It was on a Thursday,' continued Mr. Maly triumphantly.

The Count did not answer.

'I am here on business,' said Mr. Maly. 'I am going home tomorrow. Are you here on business, too?'

'No.'

'Excuse me for asking this, but I am very interested. Why have you come to Prague? You are such an interesting man. I thought so at once when I saw you the other day.'

The Count stuck his eyeglass under his pointed brow.

'I came here for health reasons,' he replied.

'Did you really? That's amazing. But you look so well. Of course, I know appearances are not everything. But even so. Excuse me, and how long are you going to stay?'

'As long as the air suits me.'

'The air? But the air is not good here at all. Now if it is air you want, you should go to Karlsbad. Do you know it? Wonderful place. And very exclusive.'

'I have no desire to go there.'

'But you are wrong to say that, you don't know it. Of course, it is expensive. Every breath you take costs money. It is very well worth it, though. I'll tell you what I'll do. I will write to the manager of the Imperial – I know him personally – and he will give you a fine room.'

'Don't trouble.'

'Don't say that, I don't mind the trouble at all. I am glad to be of help to you, Count Szalay. There is something else I wanted to ask you. Do you know the Steinborns? Baron Ludwig Steinborn? They have an estate near Pardubice, that's where I live. Very big estate.'

'I don't know them.'

'You don't? That's amazing. I thought you would.'

'Why should I?'

'They are very well known.'

'It depends to whom,' replied the Count.

'I know them,' said their hostess who had stepped nearer. Hedwig and the Professor remained talking by the window.

'That is to say, I used to know the family years ago,' added Steffanie. 'Does that please you? And now come and sit down beside me and don't torture the Count with your questions any more. The Count is something of a mystery man and if you persist with your questions, he may suddenly disappear through the wall, the way ghosts do, and my maid would give me notice. So have a heart, Mr. Maly.'

'You interest me, madam,' said the Count, as he drew up a chair and sat down. 'I think it is my turn to ask questions now.'

'I was only giving way to my silly fancies,' replied Steffanie. 'But I always took it for granted that you were dead. Does this surprise you?'

'Not in the least. Beautiful women are always uncharitable!' he answered coldly. 'You have probably heard of my two brothers who fell in the war and thought of them.'

'I knew about that. And I also knew that the third one – I mean you – was killed. I talked about you only the other day, because, as Mr. Maly here says, you are such an interesting man, so you will understand. As I was saying, I was not alone in my delusion because old Colonel Vitasek thought the same as I did. He was quite positive about it that you were dead. Although I am really very glad that you are here to contradict me, because one live man is better than two dead Counts.'

'I was reported missing in nineteen hundred and seventeen, during the campaign in the Dolomites.'

'Ah, that explains it. Now you have earned your right to drink tea with us, Count Szalay. And when I say tea, it is not really tea because I have ordered iced coffee.' And Steffanie rang for the maid.

The blonde and smiling Katy appeared, holding a tray of filled coffee glasses; her white and crisply pleated cap was no less appetizing than the bowl of whipped cream which she placed on the sofa table. On a platter, *petit fours* were piled up in rising circles, their rounded polls glazed with layers of rosy and cinnamon-coloured sugar, so that they looked like a minute Byzantine church composed of many cupolas. There was a tall sponge cake, baked in the shape of a crown, with a yellow inside marbled with veins of chocolate.

Katy cut the cake and offered it round, with a marked intention to linger when she was bending over the men's shoulders and she broke into a delighted giggle when Mr. Maly entreated her to choose the nicest slice for him.

'Like master like dog,' murmured the Count who was sitting next to Hedwig.

Professor Surovy crumbled his cake with slow and deliberate movements and holding his coffee glass delicately, as though it were a glass of wine, he began to discourse, for no apparent reason, of his student days in Paris.

'Whenever I see a well-set table like this, I am reminded of the afternoon tea which I had to provide once, as a young man in Paris. It was the first exhibition of my pictures which I had planned, and it had to be in my studio, as no art gallery would have lent itself for that purpose – to my great indignation, as you can imagine. My pictures, well, I thought they would form the main attraction, but my friends more farseeing than I was, urged me to serve refreshments as well. The invitations had already been sent out. If all went well, I had to expect about one hundred people. That meant tea for a hundred. Where was it to come from?' The Professor paused and looked round. Everybody was looking at him with an expectant smile.

'I shudder when I think of my impertinence in those days. I had no money, of course, and no connections. So I went to a shop two doors away from the house where I lived. It was a butcher's shop and they also sold cooked meats, hams, jellies and the like. There I went. Can you furnish me with a complete afternoon tea for a hundred people? I said to the proprietor, sandwiches and all? To my amazement he received my query with great composure. He did not even ask if I could pay for it, he knew me too well for that. It depends, he said. If I like your stuff, you shall have the tea. He came to my studio there and then, stood about in his white apron and judged the paintings. I got my tea. And strangely enough, the show was a success. Several people bought. My well-meaning friends were of the opinion that the oxen which the good butcher had slain must have been the forefathers of the persons who bought.'

'Excuse me, and did you feel quite well afterwards?' asked Mr. Maly. 'You see, I am asking this, because I fell ill when I was in Paris. It was a food poisoning. I had eaten some ham in just such a shop as you mentioned. Perhaps it was the same shop, I wonder? I can't tell you the name of the street, but I would find it again, it was off the Boulevard Raspail. So I went to a doctor. A French doctor, of course, a very famous man, he had been specially recommended to me. Doctor, it was something in the ham, I said. No doubt about it, he replied, there is always something in the ham, otherwise people would not eat it. And for that piece of nonsense I had to pay him his fee. I never went to Paris again. I had had quite enough.'

The talk continued about Paris, which is always a rewarding subject.

The table was cleared and soon afterwards Hedwig and the Count rose to go. Mr. Maly, too, got ready to leave. While they were saying their goodbyes, Richard Marek was shown into the room, followed by Katy with a glass of iced coffee.

'Steffanie, I kiss your hand. Hedwig, you are on the move already? What's the matter? What's the hurry? And dragging all the men away with you? With the exception of the Professor. Naturally. He is old enough to know better.'

'We are going to the opera tonight,' said Hedwig, 'so we have got to be at home in time to change. And we can take Mr. Maly with us in the car and drop him at his hotel. There is just time for it, if we go straight away.'

'Go ahead. Give my regards to your mother. I'll call on her some time or other.'

As soon as the three visitors were gone, Steffanie leaned prettily against the mauve and yellow striped silk cushions of the small settee and placed her hand over its arm, which was inlaid with ebony rosettes.

The Professor sat down in a wing chair which had a zig-zag embroidery of rainbow tints, while Richard Marek, with the freedom allowed to the constant visitor, remained standing by the window with his glass in his hand. For a while there was the rather satisfied and intimate silence, which is so often produced when a party has broken up and only a few close friends remain behind.

'So we are going to the opera tonight,' began Richard Marek. 'We. Did you hear it, Steffie? First out to tea together and then to the opera. What do you make of it, Steffie?'

'The obvious. But I need not have heard this last remark. I could have told you before. One look at Hedwig, *et voilà*. She sits there in her little blue frock and the little white collar as good as gold, of course, and as quiet as usual, just the way Melanie trained her to be. But the face above the little collar does not fit any more. I could not tell you how she has changed, but her face is softer and there is something in her eyes – but then, there is always something in everybody's eyes, as Mr. Maly's French doctor would have probably said. I just don't know what it is, but I do know why.'

'Yes, yes, you are right, Steffanie.'

''Of course I am right. But you are only saying this, Richard, so that I should stop talking about it. Do you mean perhaps that it is not my business?'

'I could hardly say that, Steffanie, especially as you seem to have made it your business already. I thought it was all Melanie's doing. But from what you say, the girl is head over heels in love with him. I did not think it was possible.'

'Everything is possible. And why not, I ask you?'

'Oh, I don't know,' and with this he put his empty glass on the sill, stroked his hair and glanced dubiously round the room.

The Professor lit a cigarette and sat still in his chair.

'You sound so bad-tempered about it, dear Richard,' began Steffanie. 'As though it seemed *contre-cœur* to you. I should have thought you would be very pleased. From the look of things, the engagement will be announced any day now. Are you annoyed, perhaps, that you were not told? Any day now, I say, and I think it is a lovely thought that Hedwig will be happy.'

'Lovely thought.'

'Is there anything on your mind?' asked Steffanie and she leaned forward and placed her long beautiful hand on her breast as though to persuade him of her genuine concern. 'I am sorry we are so boring, Professor,' she said in a more ordinary tone of voice.

'I am a cross between a piece of furniture and a family physician, dear madam. And, as you know, I never talk out of school. I am a great believer in discretion, in life as well as in art. *Ars celare artem.*'

'You are kind. Well, speak up now, Richard, and say something reasonable.'

'Reasonable. What is reasonable? I don't know myself. I cannot tell you exactly what I feel. Nobody can understand me in this except Joseph, and he does not understand me either. I'll tell you how it is. I have never had a plaster cast but suppose I did break an arm and had it put in plaster and then one day I got an itch on the skin under the cast and I wanted to scratch it, but could not reach to it. That's how I feel about Ferdinand.'

'You are in doubt about him, Richard?'

'I am and then again I am not. I have no grounds whatever. And he is a born charmer. Funny, you know. When I am with him, I could eat out of his hand. That is, if he wanted me to, of course. And when I am away from him and someone mentions his name, I am on my guard at once and expect to hear – but what do I expect to hear, for heaven's sake? He is not a criminal and he is not a scoundrel and even if he were, I should not blink an eyelash because I know that he would be a scoundrel with kid gloves and with a kiss-your-hand manner. He has no money. And why should he have? Richer people than he go begging nowadays. And I enquired if they knew him at the Jockey Club in Vienna, and they did, and said he has been most correct in all his dealings. And yet – I just don't feel easy, somehow.'

'I don't either,' replied Steffanie. 'I tried to pull the worms out of his nose, as the saying goes, today, but he had an answer to everything. And a very good answer, very plausible. And just because of it, I did not like it. But on the other hand, if he had not been plausible, I would have liked it even less. The more I think about it, the more my mind runs round in circles and it is all probably a silly prejudice on my part. You know how it is. When one is suspicious, everything points towards the spot which confirms one's suspicion and one leads one's self up the garden path. I don't like the man. That's all.'

'If I may be very outspoken, dear madam?'

'Yes, Professor?'

The old man adjusted his pince-nez with great deliberation before he spoke. 'You are used to seeing all of us at your feet, dear madam, and quite rightly so. But Count Szalay has always been cold to your charms. Does not the explanation for your dislike lie there?'

'How ridiculous!' exclaimed Steffanie, and she sat up straight and smoothed the folds of her black and white checked taffeta skirt with a movement which was curiously prim and abrupt.

'Not a bad guess, Professor,' said Richard Marek. 'Steffanie likes to attract men, it is the breath of life to her. She will probably answer that she has got enough admirers already, but that is not strictly true. Two crowns are better than one and ten better than two. Aren't I right, Steffie?'

'You are absurd, Richard. As though I cared. Besides, you are doubtful about the Count yourself.'

'That makes no difference, Steffanie.'

'And why not?'

'Because I am a fool.'

CHAPTER 19

It was eleven o'clock in the morning. In the hot yard, Rollo was walking round the acacia tree and pretending to follow a scent; from time to time he turned his twitching nostrils towards the kitchen and, with eyes shining like emeralds, he sniffed the odours of roasting meat. At last, he sat down and had a hearty scratch.

The cook stood at the kitchen table, with her arms buried up to the elbows in an earthenware vessel filled with dough, in which bubbles rose and burst at each kneading movement.

Joseph, standing by the window in shirtsleeves and without his neckcloth, gave a last polish to his master's riding boots and occasionally wiped his face on the blue and white curtains, with a furtive glance towards the cook.

'They can't do without me,' he said. 'Tomorrow afternoon they start with the decorations and then I'll have to have a talk with their footman. I'll give him the once over and get him organized. Organization is very important. That's what divides people into classes, the upper and the lower ones.'

'What do you want to do with him?' growled the cook. 'You take one tray and he takes the other. The work's got to be done and you can't organize it away, the way I see it,' and she turned angrily towards him and threw him a furious glance beneath thick black eyebrows. Although the red and cracked skin of her forehead was streaked with flour, her countenance was as imperious as ever. Joseph turned his back on her and straightened the curtain with hasty fingers.

'That footman of theirs is no good. I knew it as soon as I set eyes on him. He's got pimples all over his face.'

'If he had the choice he would not have them,' retorted the cook and slapped the dough with an expression of ill temper.

Joseph put the boots and the brush down and leaned against the dresser with crossed arms. 'Mr. Simek is already there,' he remarked. 'He will be there for five days.'

'That's the worst of weddings, food and food again. Personally, I prefer a funeral. That's more refined.' She turned the dough out of the bowl, cut it in nine equal parts with the speed and accuracy born of a lifetime's experience and ran her commanding eyes over the piles of raisins, grated almonds and shredded sugared orange peel which lay on the marble slab.

'Everything will have to be planned to a routine,' said Joseph. 'It's going to be the biggest wedding of the year. What with Mr. Simek and myself – and working for a Hungarian. If I had known that it would come to this, when I first saw him outside the door, I would have——'

'What would you have done? You would have opened the door for him just the same and taken his card just the same, and bowed him out just the same. And why can't you leave him alone? A fine gentleman like him and always pleasant and when he likes a sauce he sends a message that he likes it, and does not shovel his food in without noticing what's on

169

his plate and never so much as a thank you.' With this, she grasped the rolling pin in such a threatening way, that many people would have taken to their heels and run for dear life.

Joseph sneered: 'He sends you his compliments because he can't afford a tip. I know his kind. He is no good, I tell you. None of the Hungarians are. If it had not been for them, we would not have lost the war.'

'Leave me alone with your war. Decent people never make such a fuss about it. When I was in service in Vienna during the war, there was a scare that the Russians were coming. The porter's wife was in hysterics and all the others with no breeding. But my madam was as cool as could be. That's where breeding shows. If the Russians come, she said to me, show them into the drawing-room and give them tea. Then they will go away again. It's not my war, it's the Emperor's war, and I am Mrs. Richter and I did not start it. That's how decent people behave. And why shouldn't the Count marry Miss Hedwig? He is in love with her and he's got his feelings, same as everybody else.' She seized four of the strips of dough and began to braid them into a plait.

'He does not love her. He loves her money,' said Joseph.

'The way you talk,' replied the cook, 'Every gipsy tells fortunes after his own stars and you think of nothing but tips, so you think everybody else does, too. He loves her all right. I have been thinking it over and I know why.' She dipped her hands into the raisins and sprinkled them over the cake with large and generous movements.

'It's because of the Baroness,' she continued. 'She is like a witch, only that witches ride away on their broomsticks and she doesn't. She is here all the time. Only the other day she comes in here and wants a recipe. Madam, that recipe belonged to my old mistress and I won't let go of it, I said, I am not a traitress I said, and I don't dish out recipes like they do carrots on the market. She flounced out again, but I had to sit down afterwards and was all in a tremble. Now don't you tell me your wicked stories. If it was the money he is after, he wouldn't get married, when he knows he'll have the Baroness for breakfast, lunch, and dinner. No money in the world would make him put up with her, mark my word. It's real love the way I see it. And he such a gentleman.'

'You'd be surprised what gentlemen will do for money,' replied Joseph.

'Maybe I would and maybe I wouldn't. And now get out of my kitchen seeing that you've done the boots, or I'll surprise you and you won't like it.'

CHAPTER 20

THE FIRST ACT of the *Fledermaus* was nearing its end.
On the stage the singing teacher, a gross young tenor,
supped with Rosalinde, after having put on her husband's
cap and housegown. The governor of the prison made his
entry in white tie and tails and invited him with great polite-
ness to follow him to what he referred to as his 'Dove cot'.
A few more duets with a brandishing of champagne glasses,
the two men made their exit, the curtain fell. The lights
went up. In their family box in the dress circle, Miss Kreslov
and her sister sat side by side on the spidery gilded chairs.
They both wore white period dresses with rows of frills
from waist to hem. Hedwig had peeled off the fingers of her
long white gloves and rolled them round her wrists. Behind
her chair, with gleaming eyeglass and pearl studs, stood
Count Szalay.

In the background Fräulein Lotte rose from the small red
plush settee which stood alongside the oblique partition
wall. 'Now come along, Ali,' she said. Already she had
fastened the modest seal-skin collar of her coat and taken
Alexandrine's wrap from the hook.

'I don't see why I should go, Fräulein,' said Alexandrine

without turning round, as she clutched the pair of opera glasses on the red plush balustrade.

'It's not suitable that you should stay, Ali.'

'But I know what is going to happen, I know the whole piece,' and Alexandrine began to sob.

'Of course you do, but it's not proper that you should see it. And let go of the opera glasses, they only spoil your eyes.' With this and several more admonitions and encouragements, Fräulein Lotte got her charge out of the box. It was an occurrence to which she was well accustomed.

The Baroness believed in the educating influence of good music and good plays but she also believed in early bedtime hours for children. Thus Fräulein Lotte knew by heart the first acts of all the well-known operas, without ever having witnessed their endings.

'In a way these precautions with young girls are quite useless,' said the Count above Hedwig's shoulder. 'If they do understand the jokes, well and good, and if they don't, all the better. Still, appearances have to be kept. But apart from this, it would not hurt Alexandrine to stay up till eleven at night once in a while.' He paused. 'Is there anyone you wanted to see or would you rather stay here?'

'I'd rather stay here, Ferdinand,' said Hedwig. She turned half way to him and tapped with her programme on the balustrade. 'You won't sit down? No, I know you never do,' she added, somewhat breathlessly.

She gave a little laugh. 'You will probably quite soon get used to our opera routine; I think I never was as bad as Alexandrine, but taken all in all, the scenes enacted in our box were sometimes more dramatic than those on the stage.' She turned away from him and looked in front of her, at the three tiers of boxes opposite, dipped in the discreet and ruddy glow of red plush hangings, each flanked by a pair of gilded cherubs holding a lamp shaped like a torch.

'And now, Ferdinand, I must ask you something. You are not a Count, are you?'

She could hear the rustle of his shirt front. Then silence. Then his voice, cool and slightly supercilious: 'And?'

'There is no and, I have no proof. I don't need it because I know. I mean, I don't want to question you. There is nothing else I wanted to say.'

She remained as she was, with her back turned towards him. She felt that he was bending over her shoulder: 'So the dance is at an end?' And speaking still more closely: 'Or isn't it?'

'One does not abandon one's partner in the middle of the dance floor – Count Szalay. Surely I don't have to tell you that.' She put the programme on the balustrade and twisted herself round, facing him. They smiled at each other.

'It would have been a pity to stop,' he replied. 'Especially as the orchestra is so willing to play.'

'Yes,' she said, and began to laugh. 'Oh God, when I think of it. And Mama.'

She rose from her chair and stepped before the mirror to arrange her hair. Above her head, a gilded cherub held a round white lamp, which poured its milky light onto the glass and the scrolled rococo frame, formed of an extravagant vegetation of leaves and tendrils.

'Shall we go outside and smoke?' she asked.

'With the greatest pleasure.'

They stepped into the passage and began to pace up and down after having lighted their cigarettes. They were alone except for the toothless black-robed woman who kept the keys of the boxes and one of the liveried attendants who stood together in a niche in front of a pier table.

Hedwig took the Count's arm. She was in high spirits. 'I am sorry if I scared you. Did I?' she asked.

'You gave me a very uncomfortable moment.'

'I am really very sorry, Ferdinand. But you see, I had to ask you. I had to know – the wedding is two days ahead – you understand, don't you?'

'Of course I do. The feeling that one is more clever than anybody else is irresistible. And you are very clever, Hedwig. I never underrated your intelligence. That is why I did let you have some insight into my real life before. Some, but not enough, as it turns out now. I suppose that it was at the tea party at Steffanie Smejkal's that you had your first doubt?'

'Oh no, Ferdinand,' said Hedwig and looked at him with a proud and tender smile. 'I began to wonder much earlier than this. You see, there was nothing for me to fasten on to. On the contrary, there was the "all round" – I mean Uncle Richard. He knew you and you knew him. You exchanged memories, you recalled things which you could not have possibly invented.'

'Of course not, my dear child. Those memories, they were all true. My mother knew your uncle – intimately, if I may say so. She used to wash his shirts. And I grew up on the Count's estate as a stable boy.'

'Yes?'

Hedwig caught her breath. 'And it still rankles, doesn't it, Ferdinand? I have noticed it – you treat servants so badly.'

175

'Do I? Yes, perhaps I do. You are right, my dear. But that's neither here nor there. What put the idea into your charming little head? I should have thought that Mrs. Smejkal's cross-examination – but you say it was not that?'

'Oh no, Ferdinand.' And she turned her happy, flushed face to him. 'That only showed me how you arranged things. But I felt the whole time that you were playing a part. You were too much at your ease, too accomplished somehow. And then I said to myself: what is he pretending? You are so handsome, Ferdinand, so attractive – yes, you know you are. But that does not count for anything in our society. Your only asset with us – with Mama I mean and the others – was your good name. As soon as I realized that, I knew it all.' She stopped and put her hand on his arm. 'You are not angry with me, are you? I shall never tell anybody, you know that.'

'And Mama least of all,' he said, looking into her eyes with cool amusement.

'Mama. Imagine it!' she said delightedly.

He offered her another cigarette. The first bell rang. They began to pace up and down again.

'I admire your delicacy of feeling,' said the Count. 'Your devotion to Mama is wonderful. You want to spare her feelings. Isn't that so? Yes, yes, I know it.'

She was shaken by a fit of laughter.

The bell rang for a second time. The voices of people who were surging back into the stalls grew louder like the murmurs of a distant sea. They heard footsteps in the passage. 'Let's go in,' said the Count. 'I don't feel like meeting anybody just now. I should be unable to make them see our joke.'

176

As soon as they had returned to the box, the lights went out. Amidst a creaking of seats and rustling of programmes the curtain went up.

On the stage, the ballroom was set with a group of guests bursting into song on one side, and Prince Orlowski alone on the other. He leaned against a pillar and gazed with beautiful disdain into the audience. He was played by a famous soubrette from Vienna who was making a guest appearance in Prague. She was a stout middle-aged woman whose powerful calves bulged in the silk stockings beneath the breeches, but the ankles and the feet in the buckled shoes were surprisingly slender.

'Hem. The Kartner,' said the Count. He stuck his eyeglass under his raised brow and bent over Hedwig's chair.

'I thought she was prettier. And younger.'

'She has seen better days. Or shall I say better nights? But wait till she starts.'

Hedwig turned to the Count. He took her hand and kissed it. 'I am so happy, Ferdinand. Are you, too? I mean, after all your efforts – was it worth it?'

To her amazement he did not hasten to reply. He stroked her fingers. At last he said, 'Yes. More or less. To be frank, it is not all I had hoped for. I am told I shall have to serve an apprenticeship. I thought I would be allowed the full reins.' He paused. 'But, my dear, you are so sweet and charming that you make up for everything else. You are much more than I deserved.' All this lightly and in an undertone, so that it was impossible to tell how much sincerity was contained in his words.

And then the Kartner started. She detached herself from the pillar and advanced languidly half way across the stage.

An ineffable boredom filled her countenance. Like all accomplished actresses, she already held the audience before she had uttered a sound. She began the famous aria of the tired young worldling, wandering to and fro, seemingly at random. Suddenly she came to life. It was like a flash of lightning. By the time she had threatened to throw anyone out of the house who dared to be bored with her – Prince Orlowski's – parties, all were breathless with a mixture of fear and delight. In the end, after pronouncing her rousing '*chacun à son goût*', she shrugged, threw a champagne bucket, and smashed a few glasses for good measure. It was like watching a thunderstorm from a safe distance.

'What a temperament,' murmured the Count.

'Poor Ali. She really missed something,' said Hedwig. 'And poor Fräulein Lotte,' she added, and glanced at him sideways.

'She would have been shocked to the core by the bad example, my dear. Prince Orlowski is not a gentleman. I can just hear her. And very likely she would have been convinced, that, if she had brought up Prince Orlowski herself, this disgusting exhibition would never have happened.'

CHAPTER 21

ON A WARM and dull afternoon in the middle of October, Baron Kreslov left his business house on the Neuwags Platz and walked in the direction of the Wilson Station. He passed the beginning of the Luetzow Street with a gait which was sometimes slow and sometimes hasty and which betrayed the fact that he was not used to taking walks, and arrived at the thin railings which enclosed the Stadtpark.

He stopped in front of the open gates, started to read one of the municipal notices which were inscribed in red letters on an enamel plaque, broke off in the middle and continued on his journey.

Like all ageing business men he had been advised by his doctor to take regular exercise, an advice given with full knowledge that it would never be obeyed and therefore extremely gratifying to the physician, as it enables him to shift the blame from himself on to the patient.

The long walk of the park was straight and uninviting and lined with sickly-looking trees. On the border of the patchy lawn, dead leaves had been swept into small heaps at even intervals. The benches were empty. Governesses walked in pairs together, immersed in earnest talk, carrying hoops and toys absent-mindedly, while their charges dragged at a good distance behind, indulged in sulky grimaces, or broke into sudden frenzied runs. From time to time one of the governesses stopped and called to the children with the pained air of a queen who has to attend to a trifling but undignified task.

'I might as well do the whole round,' said the Baron to himself. He entered the main square of the park, laid out in flower beds, where the last roses and dahlias raised their meagre and bedraggled crowns. Then he turned into a narrow path and came to a standstill in front of the rusty iron fence which barred the entry to the tiny pond. At the back of the pond was an artificial rock and from its crags and crevices poured several thin waterfalls with the monotony of clockwork.

The Baron put his hands into the pockets of his loose mud coloured overcoat and looked with tired and ironic eyes at the handful of ducks which criss-crossed the murky surface. Occasionally, they lifted a wing and revealed a band of glossy steel blue which flashed on their sandy, speckled sides like the ribbon of an order. They steered slowly to the chunks of bread which were thrown to them, but most of the time failed to reach the morsels.

'Dull lot,' thought the Baron. 'They don't care. Not enough competition among them.' And he turned his back to the pond.

About ten minutes later, he entered a grey stone-faced house in the street overlooking the Stadtpark. It had a heavy carved porch, gleaming white window sashes and black iron grilles in front of the ground-floor windows.

Once inside, he crossed a round marble-paved hall with niches set with statues and palms and mounted a flight of steps which were enclosed by a scrolled balustrade and carpeted with olive green plush. At shoulder level, along the inner wall of the stairs, the loops of a thick crimson cord were fastened onto ornamental brass nails.

Hedwig opened the front door of her flat.

'Papa, how nice to see you,' and she kissed the top of his head.

She wore a very elegant black dress with a short embroidered jacket and belt. She had no jewellery, but there were small paste buckles on her pointed shoes.

'All dressed up to kill, Hedwig,' said the Baron in his comfortable rumbling voice and held her away at arm's length to have a look at her. 'And those shoes – pointed and high-heeled. Your mother would turn in her grave if she saw them, I mean if she were in her grave, but she is alive and well, of course, for which we must be thankful. When I think how you had to wear ankle boots and flat heels to strengthen your tendons or whatever God put there in His wisdom. Don't you have weak ankles any more?'

'I never noticed it. Allow me, Papa.' And Hedwig took her father's coat and hung it inside a built-in cupboard.

Although the hall was almost empty, it was imbued with the same solid and old-fashioned elegance as the entrance of the house. The doors were of glossy thick mahogany. The handles were sparkling rosettes of cut glass; and discreetly screened behind latticed brass, the steam heat radiators sent out a somewhat dry and metal-scented warmth.

'Funny that. Still, Melanie knew what she was doing. Those boots you had to wear were so ugly that one could see at a glance that they were full of virtue. Never mind.

She was a good mother to you and still is to your sister. Alexandrine can sing a song about it.'

'Come in, Papa, and be comfortable.'

'That's my intention, Hedwig. The most comfortable is always comfort. Therefore, not the big drawing-room, I know you've got one, so there is no need to sit in it. The little smoking-room, that's more to my taste. And perhaps a cup of tea, but it must be weak, or I shan't buy it. And by the way, why did you have to answer the bell yourself? Where are your fair maidens?'

'I have given them the afternoon off, Papa. We are having a dinner party tomorrow, so I thought it would be wise.'

During this, Hedwig opened a door and led her father into a narrow room furnished with a plain dark brown carpet, square low bookcases made of a tropical red streaked wood, and several square easy chairs with broad arm rests, covered in parchment coloured leather. Two logs were crossed in the unlit grate and in front of the pale marble hearth lay a black bearskin with silver claws. On the desk by the window stood a silver-framed photograph of Hedwig in evening dress, and there was a black morocco writing-case and blotting folder, both stamped in the corner in gold, with the initials F.L.G.Sz. and the nine-pointed coronet above them.

There was only one picture on the wall, painted by Professor Surovy in the pointillist manner of his youth: a group of Slovak peasant women bent over a harvest field. Their colourful pleated skirts filled the whole foreground of the painting.

The Baron folded his short hands above his stomach and wandered round the room. He stopped in front of the photograph. 'Very nice, Hedwig, makes you look like an Archduchess. Who took it? Ah, Schlosser & Wenisch. They are past masters at retouching. And that's new? I have not seen it before,' he said pointing at the folder. 'Not like Ferdinand really, to splash himself about with his high-born initials.'

'It is not his fault, father,' replied Hedwig. 'I gave these to him. As a special wedding-present,' and she turned round with a smile and began to hum the song of Prince Orlowski, '*Chacun à son goût.*'

'No offence meant against your taste, Hedwig. It's very nice really. And why shouldn't he show off his coronet? There is positively no reason why he should hide it.'

'I did not mean it that way, Papa. I just sang it because it came into my head.'

'It did, did it? As I was saying, all is very nice and very handsome. And no dust traps, that's what I like about the place. Although there is one thing in the house which shows that you have not entirely forgotten your home.'

'And that is, father?'

'The palms downstairs,' and he chuckled.

'Oh, those. I wish the porter would remove them. But he won't. They are the apple of his eye, Papa. To me they are more like a thorn, if you want to know the truth.'

'Haha, I thought so. You can't fool me. Now what about some tea?'

Hedwig went out and he sat down in one of the chairs opposite the picture. 'Queer, these Slovak wenches,' he said to himself, 'the richer they are, the more skirts they wear, one on top of the other and when they walk they flap up and down like the colours of the rainbow. Very pretty. And very reasonable really, you count their skirts and you know where you are with them. You got so many skirts? Right you are, you shall have credit. And so on. But with us, it would not do. With Melanie it's jewellery instead, but she could even wear sham diamonds and people would take it for granted that they were real. In the long run it all becomes pointless. Funny, that.'

Hedwig returned. 'It will be ready in a minute, Papa. The cook was a bit offended,' she continued with the happy complacency of the young married woman who still finds pleasure in the running of her household. 'It is not really her job to make tea. That's not cooking.'

'Offended, was she? Tell the mimosa I will make it worth her while. They are all the same. The less they are, the more they stand on their dignity. Now I, for instance, I don't care what I do – if it was not for my weak stomach. Or take your husband, for example. The other day there was a rush to get some samples off and he went downstairs himself and helped with the packing. That's the sort of man he is. He is a remarkable fellow, Hedwig.'

'Yes, yes, Papa.'

'You say that like this, Hedwig, as though I were telling you a home truth. You only know him from your side and, of course, you think the world of him when you see him here or in company. And he is a charmer, don't I know it. But in my part of the world you don't know him at all, Hedwig, there you must take my word for it and that's why I came here today to tell you, because generally I never see you on your own. I am going across now, I said to him this afternoon, you coming along? But not he. There was a meeting here and a report there and you won't see him till he has sat it through. And when I say, sat it through, that is not doing him justice either, he is as sharp as a needle and when he does not get an answer straight away, he goes and finds out for himself. And he calculates and looks round the corner, if that does make any sense to you. He's got the makings of a big business man, Hedwig.'

'I can quite see it, Papa. He does not leave anything to chance.'

'Exactly. And if there is no chance, he makes it. I am most agreeably disappointed in him, if you know what I mean. After all, he has learnt nothing but horsemanship and sol-diering and I thought when I took him on, that he was one of those pleasant fellows who are good at everything except making their own living. He is a fine person, Hedwig.'

'Yes, Papa. I am glad you think so.'

The tea was carried in by the cook, a grey-haired, small emaciated woman with a suffering face who, with her clean white linen coat and severe countenance, looked like a sick-nurse.

'My word!' said the Baron after she had left.

'We are all afraid of her, Papa.'

'I can see it. She gives you a queer feeling. Better keep her in the background when you have guests,' remarked the Baron and he quoted: ' "No good to unveil those dark abysses which the gods graciously cover with fear and horror." I suppose you will have Simek tomorrow?'

'Oh no, Papa. Our cook will not put up with him and he annoyed Ferdinand, you know, he was too familiar. Ferdi-nand says that I must keep more distance.'

'Don't talk to me about distance. I had a wonderful talk with Simek once, all about carps, quite philosophical. And talking of carps, that reminds me of Ferdinand. I think in six months' time I will make him chairman of one of my companies. He'll do wonders there. They need stirring up. They always put one pike into the big carp ponds to chase the carp round so that they don't get lazy and muddy. Ferdinand shall be my pike. There is something of a beast of prey about him, now that I come to think of it. In a nice way, of course. A bit savage and dashing, what? That's probably his Hungarian warrior ancestry. Funny, that I never thought of it before. Breeding will out, Hedwig.'

'So they say, Papa. Is this tea weak enough for you or shall I give you more water?'

'I'll take it as it is.'

'Here you are, Papa. But about breeding. I don't know. I certainly would not call Ferdinand savage. Do you consider it savage, if you please, to get up at the same time every morning and to be at the office at ten o'clock sharp? The world could come to an end, but you still would find him at ten in the Heuwags Platz. And the rest follows. He turns down a little shooting party at the Birks' lodge near Kirna, because he cannot spare the time. Do you call that dashing? And old Mr. Birk makes a crack, you know how tactless he is, and asks me if you have chained Count Szalay to your money bags and while I go red and white with embarrassment, Ferdinand simply laughs and say, yes, as though this was the most natural thing in the world. At the house ball at the Ribeks', he is barely dashing enough to stay for one hour and then he goes home, very savagely, I daresay, and sends the car for me. And when we are invited, he thinks twice before accepting, dashing as he is, because he hates late hours and gets up at six every day to get his ride in the Baumgarten. I have now returned to the company of Mr. Robinson, if you want to know.'

The Baron put his cup down. 'Yes, yes,' he said, and was silent. 'That's life,' he added and paused again. He set an ashtray spinning like a top and remarked at last: 'That's how it is, you know.'

Hedwig did not answer and looked into the bottom of her teacup with the obstinate expression she used to wear when her mother harangued her.

'And anyway, what's wrong with Mr. Robinson?' asked the Baron with great good humour. 'It is his job to ride out with you, he is paid for it. You would not want Ferdinand to play his role, would you? Be reasonable, Hedwig. If he did, you would be the first to despise him. Be thankful he did not turn out to be a waster. You would not have liked that, would you?'

She remained silent.

'You would not have liked it at all, take my word for it. And what do you expect from the poor man, I should like to know. Is he to go out with the hounds and the horns and shoot you another bear like the one you've got on the floor, which he has already done once, so there is positively no reason why he should do it again. He has got other sports now, if you look at it in the right way. I cannot imagine anything more like a jungle than the Stock Exchange: you can be stabbed in the back and scalped alive there, just as though you were among Red Indians. Do you think I got my weak stomach for nothing?'

'Poor father.'

'And talking of Red Indians, Melanie is on the warpath again. She is getting her lists ready. The concert, you know.'

'Is a date fixed for it yet, Papa?'

'I think so. Early January, I believe. Ali is to sell programmes for the first time. And we shall all listen to music and drink champagne so that the poor children can go on a holiday in summer.'

'I shall not raise a finger this time, Papa. I don't feel charitable,' said Hedwig.

'So I have noticed. Still, never mind. I am keeping out of this. You fight it out with your mother.'

'I shall not, Papa,' replied Hedwig. 'I shall just say that I won't do it. Why should I have to fight? I am grown up now and if I am old enough to be married, I am old enough to know my own mind. Don't you agree?'

'Old enough is always a ticklish question with Melanie. When it suited her, you were old enough not to believe in Father Christmas and on the other hand you were not old enough to do what you wanted. Leave me out of this.'

'Very well, Papa. I shall speak to Mama when the time comes.'

'Good idea. All very nice, but I must be going now.'

Hedwig saw him to the door with a smile.

Afterwards she stood for a while by the window and watched the uneven gait of her father in his mud-coloured topcoat. The street lighter crept along the pavement with his long pole and every time he stopped, a lantern glimmered beneath the black trees. The sky was still white, but already the room sank into darkness and the streaks in the bookcases along the walls stood out so vividly, that it seemed as though red and yellow flames were burning into the wood.

CHAPTER 22

RICHARD MAREK had introduced him to his Club and taken him to the coffee-house. The Baroness had given two dinners for him. He had been to the opera and had drank tea with Steffanie Smejkal. Count Szalay had driven him to the castle in Melnik and to the lake in Jevany. Hedwig and Fräulein Lotte had shown him the Town Hall and the clock striking at noon, when the twelve apostles come out of the turret one by one and nod their heads, the iron cock crows, the Turk rattles his sabre, and Death shakes his scythe. He had visited the monastery in Strahov and admired the frescoes in the library.

They all agreed that he was a very nice man and consoled themselves with the thought that his visit would soon come to an end.

His name was William John Herring, of Herring & Sons, Ltd., timber merchants in Cheapside in the City of London, where Rudy Kreslov served as a junior assistant. His business trip had taken him to Sweden and Finland, the Baltic States, Poland, and finally to Prague. He was a lanky, phlegmatic man of about thirty-five. His straight black hair grew low on his forehead. He had green eyes, long thin lips, and a long chin.

Hedwig watched him across the dining table with a slight look of impatience as he lounged in his chair and filled the room with the foreign aroma of his pipe.

'A drop more coffee?' she asked.

'No thank you. It is too good. I still can't get used to it.'

'Ferdinand?'

'No thank you, my dear.'

'In that case,' said Hedwig, 'I think we had better go. If we get there too late, it will be full.'

'Certainly, my dear.'

They all rose. 'I think you will like it, Mr. Herring,' said Hedwig hurriedly. 'I'll put my coat on. I shan't be long.' She nodded and slipped out of the room.

The men went into the adjoining smoking-room.

'What would you like to drink?' asked the Count.

'Nothing at all, thank you very much. I had too much beer at lunch. And now the wine. It makes me feel so heavy.'

'Do you find Prague very tiring? Many people do.'

'I think it is the pavements. The cobblestones, you know. And the air.'

'Yes, I can imagine it,' said the Count. 'Would you rather not go out at all?'

'Oh no. I am very keen to see it. I enjoy everything. So long as I can just sit and watch,' replied Mr. Herring with an uneasy smile.

'Don't worry,' said the Count. 'You will not be expected to dance. I must confess I am rather lazy myself.'

'Are you? I am so glad.' With this the Englishman moved to the fireplace and leaned against the mantelpiece, drawing at his pipe, while his eyes sought those of the Count.

'What is worrying you?' asked the Count, and sat on the desk.

'You won't leave me alone there?'

'Of course not. You are our guest and we are glad of your company. What makes you think so badly of us?' And he turned to the other with his inward smile.

'I went out yesterday afternoon with Mr. Marek, you see. He is very kind the way he bothers with me. He took me to the Café Astor. I did not realise it all at first, I am afraid I am a bit slow.'

'I see. And did you make – an acquaintance?'

'I refused to. It was terribly embarrassing. Mr. Marek thought that I was only shy and he kept pressing me to pick up a woman. But I was not shy. I just did not feel like it. I sometimes do. But not always. You see what I mean?'

'Perfectly. I must apologize for Hedwig's uncle. I am afraid his ideas of entertaining young men are a bit hackneyed. But let me assure you, that nothing is further from my mind. This whole night club idea is really Hedwig's. A night club to her is paradise. She was never allowed to go to these places before, and now that she is married she feels she must make up for lost time. If you want to know the truth, you are merely serving as an excuse for going there. Does this reassure you?'

Hedwig entered. Under the meshes of the black veil, her face was pale. Her black velvet coat was open and the brocade lining glittered at each of her small restless movements.

'Are you ready?' she asked.

'I was just telling Mr. Herring that you are entirely responsible for whatever he is about to suffer, my dear.'

'Mr. Herring cannot leave Prague without having been to the Elysée. Rudy is bound to ask him.'

'There you are. What did I tell you? Any excuse will do,' remarked the Count and looked at the Englishman with a raised eyebrow. He took his wife's arm. She did not glance at him.

CHAPTER 23

THE ELYSÉE was situated in the basement of one of the big old hotels. A string of mauve lights flashed the letters of its name across the discreet ancient façade and beneath the glare the gold-frogged uniforms of the two porters, stationed by the revolving doors, were dulled to a livid silver.

'Our Heaven has two Saint Peters, as you see,' remarked the Count, as they went in. 'And now for the angels. We are rather well known to the angels, as you will see. Hedwig is on an excellent footing with them, aren't you, my dear?'

Hedwig smiled absent-mindedly and glanced at herself in one of the pink-tinted mirrors which framed the entrance to the stairs.

'The Turkish room is the nicest, don't you think?' she asked her husband as they descended the steps.

'Whichever you say, my dear.'

They went through a tiny bar, decorated in Austrian peasant style, with beer barrels serving as tables and crudely coloured wooden figures standing on carved shelves between pewter jugs. The walls were filled with inscriptions in Gothic lettering, exhorting the reader to drink and forget the morrow. At the door of the main room they were met by the *maître d'hôtel* and two waiters.

'Madame's favourite table is reserved.'

'What did I tell you?' murmured the Count.

In a narrow circle of flame-coloured light a Spanish dancer twisted her arms round her writhing body as though wrapping herself in an invisible veil. Nobody paid any attention to her. The band played slowly and looked dazed. A large party seated at a table near the wall laughed and talked loudly above the clatter of the castanets.

They were led through a gangway of tables and passed beneath an archway into a third room which was lit by hanging lanterns of pierced bronze. The divans and the walls above them were covered with oriental rugs and there were a number of brass and ebony tables, inlaid with ivory and mother-of-pearl.

'The seats are very soft,' said the Count. 'And that is something. Otherwise, all I can say is, if we ever come to London, I hope you will not do unto us as we have done unto you.'

'I am enjoying it,' replied the Englishman.

They sat down at a table in a corner, opposite the entrance. The Count ordered champagne.

'I think it's very nice. It is, isn't it?' said Hedwig, turning to their guest. 'Ferdinand always talks about it as though it were the Siberian salt mines.'

'I am quite content, my dear, so long as there is no forced labour.'

Mr. Herring smiled. Hedwig looked annoyed.

A pale and puny boy in a tight-fitting livery brought silver dishes with olives, potato crisps and salted almonds. The *maître d'hôtel* made his entry, guiding the trolley which was pushed by a waiter. The champagne was poured out with that unfurling of white napkins and that display of rounded, careful movements, which is the tribute accorded only to expensive wine.

They raised their glasses in silence and Hedwig looked round the room with a moody expression. The Englishman continued to drink and smoke calmly and make an occasional short remark. It was impossible to say whether he ignored the tension between his hosts, or pretended to ignore it.

From the ball-room came the sound of feeble applause. The light turned white and brilliant and the band struck up a brisk and brassy tune. They could see a part of the floor, framed by the archway and several dancing couples passing in and out of their field of vision.

A tall young man came in, paused for a while and looked at their table. Hedwig raised her head and smiled at him. He came slowly towards them, with a peculiarly graceful step. His evening suit was cut in such a way as to exaggerate the breadth of his shoulders and the smallness of his hips. He had smooth sandy hair and a smooth face, deep-set blue eyes and long, girlish eyelashes. He had the arrogance of youth but none of its uncertainty and although his face was not lined, it seemed to have lost its freshness.

'Is he a friend of yours?' asked the Englishman after some hesitation.

'I should say so,' answered the Count under his breath. 'He is what I should call the Archangel. The angel of deliverance.'

The young man approached, bowed first to the Count with a wary glance and bowed again, more deeply, to Hedwig, after having inclined his head in front of the Englishman.

'Good evening, sir. I kiss your hand, madam. Would the

Countess care to dance?' He laid his hand lightly on the back of the Count's chair, crossed his feet and bent forward in an attitude of familiarity and haughtiness.

'Good evening, George,' said the Count without moving. 'This is Mr. Herring, a friend of ours from London. Won't you sit down with us and have a glass?'

'It is very kind of you to ask me, sir, but I would rather not. Perhaps later, if we keep as slack as we are now.' He turned to Mr. Herring: 'I have been in London, too, last year in the spring. But I only stayed a month.' He gave a perfunctory smile.

'Why was that?' asked Hedwig. 'Didn't you like it?'

'I liked it well enough, madam. We put an act on at the Savoy. Then we struck bad luck. My partner became – incapacitated, so she could not go on.' Above her head he threw a knowing glance at her companions.

'What was the matter with her?' asked Hedwig.

'A weak heart,' replied the Count quickly. 'Isn't that right, George?'

'Absolutely, sir.'

'But how can you know, Ferdinand?' exclaimed Hedwig. 'Is it true, George?'

'My wife likes to get to the core of everything,' remarked the Count. 'And now, my dear, don't waste George's time. He cannot stand here and chat all evening.'

'May I go, Ferdinand?'

'Of course you may. Mr. Herring and I have to discuss some business matters which would only bore you.'

Hedwig got up quickly. As usual when she tried to hide her animation, she put on a severe face. Her companions rose for an instant, and resumed their seats.

'George is a Godsend,' remarked the Count. 'I always wonder what he talks about with the women, because whenever I look, I see they are babbling away like merry brooks. I daresay it is a professional secret. One swallow does not make a summer and good looks alone don't make a gigolo.'

'Do you pay him?' asked Mr. Herring.

'I don't have to, because he is really provided by the management for the relief of husbands – but I do give him a warm handshake, of course, at the end of an evening. He likes to pretend that this is the only source of his income and I don't feel like letting him down on it.'

'Hem!' said Mr. Herring.

As soon as they were on the dance floor, George put his arm around Hedwig's shoulder with that serious and cold attention which men assume when they are doing their work. They danced the first few steps without speaking.

At last he said: 'Shall I show you a new step? I will do it slowly at first, there is no need to worry, and then we'll do it so that the Count can see us. It looks very effective, he will like it. Won't he, madam?'

'I am sure he will,' replied Hedwig with a frown.

'Very well. Shall we try?' and suddenly he drew her closer, whirled her round with an almost savage movement and loosened his clasp as abruptly as he had tightened it. She was slightly breathless.

'No don't,' she said. 'Or perhaps yes. I should like to try. For my own sake. My husband won't notice it in any case. I could stand on my head right here and he would not look up.'

'That's exactly what I thought, Countess.'

'Then why did you say——?'

'One has to say something, madam. And I like all husbands. If it weren't for husbands I would be out of business. Take yourself for instance. You would not appreciate me if you were not married, would you?'

'That has nothing to do with it,' replied Hedwig and frowned. Looking down at her, the dancer saw that she tried to suppress a smile. She added: 'I just like dancing, that's all.'

'Then why dance with me, madam? The Count dances quite well although he holds too tight, but then all gentlemen do that. Yes, he dances quite well, as gentlemen go.'

'Yes, he does.'

'You should say when he does, madam. Now, let's start. One, and stop, and turn, and stop, and stop, and cross over with me, and turn. Quite easy, isn't it?'

She nodded and smiled.

They were passing the archway. The dancer cast a glance at the table in the corner in the Turkish room. The Count, with his chin on his hand, was listening intently to the Englishman, who had turned his back to the dance floor, with his legs stretched out comfortably; he was tapping his pipe against the sole of his foot.

'You look so sad, Countess.'

'Do I?' asked Hedwig. Up till then she had been smiling but at once she assumed a melancholy expression, as George had expected her to do. He knew from experience that as soon as a woman is told that she looks sad, she cannot resist playing up to the idea.

'And yet you look lovely this evening in your pretty new dress. I am sure I am not the first one tonight to tell you so.'

Hedwig looked in the direction of the Count's table and remained silent.

'I am sure the English gentleman is in big business,' continued George. 'He has that look about him. It seems a pity to come here and not to take any notice of what's going on. But still, there is no accounting for taste. When I was in London, there was a famous scientist who came every night to the Savoy and worked out his formulas at a table near the band. He said the noise helped him with his work. Perhaps the Count and his friend feel the same way.'

'Perhaps,' said Hedwig.

'If I were in your place, Countess, I'd soon make them snap out of it.' He paused and as Hedwig did not reply, he continued: 'But I am afraid – yes, it looks to me very much like it – yes. Ah well. Never mind.'

'What?' asked Hedwig.

'No, Countess. I won't say it. I don't want to annoy you.' He replied with an arrogance which gave the lie to his words.

'Oh, please tell me, George. I will be annoyed if you don't.'

'I said you should make them sit up and take an interest in you. But I think now that you are past caring.'

'That is quite true,' said Hedwig.

'Ah, I knew it. But if I were you, Countess, I'd wake your husband up just the same. I would like to keep you company for a while, but the place is filling up now and I shall not be able to dance with you for the next hour or two. And it would be such a pity if you had to sit through the whole evening, wouldn't it?'

Hedwig returned after the dance to the table, escorted by George, who remained a pace behind her and retired without a word as soon as she was seated.

'Did you like it, my dear?' asked the Count.

'Yes, thank you,' she said curtly. She sat very still, took

199

a cigarette and refused to have her glass refilled. The band began to play a sobbing, mawkish tune. Several people, all of them middle-aged, wandered into the room and soon every divan was occupied. The rubicund squares of the rugs, and fretwork borders of ivory and ebony dividing the walls into panels, provided a rigid Byzantine background to their elderly figures, while the flashing bronze lanterns hung like stiff crowns above their heads.

The dancer made his entry again, and again he paused in the doorway. Then he went to a table in the opposite corner without glancing to his right or left.

'Will you give me the pleasure of this dance, my dear?' asked the Count. 'I am sure Mr. Herring will excuse us.'

'Oh, please go ahead. I am enjoying it all. But I can dance, too. I mean, I can walk you round, if you can put up with it.'

'It is very good of you,' said Hedwig. 'I appreciate it very much, Mr. Herring. Perhaps the next dance.'

As soon as they were on the floor, Hedwig said to her husband: 'Really, Ferdinand, your offer was a bit late in the day, wasn't it? You take me here and let me dance with that man and only when you see that he has dropped me because he has other fish to fry, you make the effort. And on top of it all, poor Mr. Herring thinks he has to be charitable and wants to sacrifice himself. If it comes to that, I had rather leave.'

'But, my dear child, I thought you liked to dance with a professional. If I had known, I would have sent him away. And why should you not dance with Mr. Herring? He is our guest and he was merely being correct.'

'That is a splendid reason for dancing with me. Correct. Ha! I like that, I must say. And what am I to do? Fall on my knees and thank him for his kindness? That is what you would expect me to do, wouldn't you? It would be so good for business and that is all you care for. And then Mr. Herring will give the firm a big order, I daresay, and you will sing a duet of *God Save the King* with him.'

'My dear child, you are being most unreasonable. You are dreadful, you women.'

'Please don't be funny at my expense. And I am only too reasonable. I wish I did not see it all so clearly. You merely took me here so that you could talk business to him and you let me dance with George to make it quite obvious that you want to get me out of the way.'

She dropped her arm from his shoulder, twisted her hand out of his and made her way across the dance floor. The Count followed.

As soon as she had reached the table, Hedwig bent over to the divan and picked up her evening bag. It was a small, oblong case formed by golden links worked like chain armour.

'You did not like the dance?' asked Mr. Herring. 'I thought it was a silly tune myself.'

'It was not a success,' said the Count who stood behind his wife.

'I say, isn't that a beautiful bag you've got?' said Mr. Herring. 'I have never seen that sort of thing before. Isn't it clever?'

'I am glad you like it,' said Hedwig. She turned and left them. The Count looked after her and sat down.

'Is your wife not feeling well?'

'There is nothing wrong with her. She will be back in a minute.'

Hedwig walked through the gangway of tables in the main room, passed through the small bar and went upstairs to the entrance of the cloakroom.

She stopped for a while and took a deep breath, looked into a mirror and smoothed her hair. The sound of music was thin and faint. Two waiters came out of a door behind her back and for a second she could hear the clatter of a scullery. She continued to arrange her hair. Downstairs the music ceased. A liveried boy appeared at the foot of the stairs, balancing a tray on one finger. She took a tortoiseshell étui out of her bag and called him.

'Will you give me a light, please?'

He struck a match with a flourish.

'And – have a cigarette yourself.'

'No thank you, madam, not while I'm on duty. But if I may, I'll keep it for afterwards.' He helped himself and looked into her face with serious attention. He did not move.

'And will you ask George to come here, please? I want to speak to him.'

The boy ran away, taking two steps at a time. Hedwig walked up and down, looking at the floor.

The boy returned. 'I am very sorry, madam, Mr. George says he can't come just now.'

'Will you tell him to come. I insist. I cannot stay here all evening.'

The music started again. She finished her cigarette, threw it on the floor and stamped on it. As soon as she saw the dancer's head and shoulders on the stairs below, she turned to the mirror and touched her hair. She only looked up when he stood beside her. He leaned against a pillar with his hands in his pockets.

She offered him a cigarette.

'No thank you, Countess. I always prefer to take the case. You wanted to speak to me?'

'I did. I have decided to go home. Will you see me home?'

'I couldn't possibly, madam. Your husband would not like it.' And he looked at her with a mixture of arrogance and familiarity.

'That is my affair. Will you get my coat, please?'

'I will get your coat if you want me to, madam. But I cannot come with you. After all, I am engaged here.'

'I see. It does not really matter.'

'It matters to me, madam. I don't like to see you go home all alone at this hour of the night. I'll speak to the porter, he will get you a cab.'

He inclined his head and went to the cloakroom. She watched him as he opened the door, disappeared and emerged, carrying the coat over his arm.

'I will come outside with you, madam.'

He left her in the hall and returned a minute later.

'The porter will call you when the cab is ready. I kiss your hand, Countess. I hope you will get home all right, I should have liked to be of more help to you. Of course, if you would come out with me one day, say, in the afternoon, I should be able to be more completely at your disposal. Perhaps you will let me know.'

Before Hedwig had realised what he was doing, he had taken her bag out of her hand, opened it and put a card inside it. He returned it to her with a bow.

'I kiss your hand, Countess.'

He left her before she could say a word.

CHAPTER 24

IT WAS the last day of October. Although the sky was pale and it was only three o'clock in the afternoon, it was so dark that it was impossible to read by daylight. There was that hushed, motionless, and menacing silence which precedes the fall of snow.

The Baroness Kreslov had just entered her daughter's flat and was now sitting on a chair in the hall; a maid kneeled in front of her and took off her galoshes. The Baroness had opened her black cloth coat and the faintly bitter smell of the mink lining rose into the dry heat. She held the palm of her hand, still in its white glove, in front of her face and inspected it with a resigned air.

Hedwig came out of the drawing-room.

'Mama! How nice to see you. Isn't it a horrible afternoon? It looks like the end of the world. I think we are going to have a snowstorm.'

'It never snows until the middle of November, Hedwig. You know that as well as I do. No, just a drift of fog and rain probably. I don't see what else there could be. But now look at this. I want you to take a good look at it.' And the Baroness held out her gloved fingers with great dignity. 'Do you see that dirt? These gloves were fresh this afternoon. This happened when I touched the railing on your stairs. Do you call this a well-kept house? I am going to speak to your porter about it, on my way out.'

'Oh don't, Mama, please. He is always so nice.'

'Somebody has got to speak to him. And you apparently don't. Do you think I enjoy doing it?'

With this, the Baroness got up, slipped her coat from her shoulders and took off her hat and gloves.

'This mirror hangs too high to be convenient. You should have it altered. I told you about it last time, but you never pay attention to what I say. And now we shall go into the dining-room. We shall want a large table.'

Hedwig followed her mother down the passage and into the room where the blue lacquered dresser, chests and cupboards enclosed within their wavy panels pyramids of painted apples, grapes and roses, like vistas of a southern flowered sky. The trestles of the oak table were clasped with thick bands of black iron and there were carved shelves set with plates and bowls of peasant ware; against the white walls, now livid in the failing light, they blossomed crudely and cheerfully with their oversized tulips and carnations.

The Baroness sat down.

'Why don't you put the light on, Hedwig? What are you waiting for?'

'Sorry, Mama.'

'That's better. Now look, here are the lists.' And the Baroness unfolded several typewritten sheets of paper. 'I have not given you a great deal. You can get through them in a fortnight. The tickets for the concert are not yet printed, but it does not matter. Once we get the subscriptions together, one of the secretaries and Fräulein Lotte will arrange the seating and send out the tickets. So you need not worry about that.'

'I don't, Mama.'

The Baroness gave her a short look and continued: 'I have had the names set out for you in good order. First, as you see, the Union Bank. They always give a lot and once you have got several large donations, you have created a good beginning and the rest of the people follow suit because they are afraid of looking stingy. So, as I said, the Union Bank first, and then, the Bank Verein, and then old Mr. Kolben of the Kolben-Danek Cables, and so on. A child of five could do it.'

'You are probably right, Mama.'

'Of course I am.'

'And for that reason I really don't see why I should do it.'

'Don't talk nonsense, Hedwig. And if it were only nonsense, it would not be so bad. But I come here specially to see you and hand it to you on a silver platter, what more could you want? And instead of thanking me, you make remarks which are altogether lacking in respect and gratitude. Yes, remarks, because what you just said was not the first one of that kind and you need not think that I don't notice them, even if I choose to pass them over in silence.'

'I had not meant to offend you, Mama.'

'What had you meant then? Now you sit there and make a sad face but I am not at all sure how much you mean it. Still, I do not wish to pursue this theme any further. Now fold the papers up so that they don't get crumpled before you are through with them. Back into their proper folds, Hedwig. Aren't you listening when I speak to you?' and she tapped with one finger on the table.

Hedwig put the sheets down and got up slowly and carefully, as though her limbs were aching. She said in a low voice: 'I shan't fold them up at all, Mama. And I shan't do it, because I don't want to have them. I don't want them, I did not ask for them, and I don't want anything to do with the whole concert.'

The Baroness clasped her hands to her throat as though she found it hard to swallow and closed her eyes for an instant. 'I am only thankful that your father is not here to hear this. And what about the poor children and their holiday? It is very sad that I should have to remind you of them.'

She looked at the ceiling and round the walls. 'You furnish this room like a farm cottage, you make yourself ridiculous with it to say the least, but when it is a question of thinking of the poor, doing something for them, that's a very different story. Everything is too much trouble for you. All is falseness and affectation.'

'Perhaps it is, Mama. But your charity affairs——'

'What about them? What have they got to do with it?'

'Nothing, Mama.' And Hedwig sat down again.

'I think you will agree that it is an excellent cause.'

'Perhaps, Mama.'

The Baroness wrenched her chair back from the table and looked her daughter full in the face with her somewhat bulging blue eyes. 'Stop saying, "perhaps Mama". It sounds more offensive than if you disagreed with me completely. If you have anything against the concert, though I cannot possibly see what it could be, tell me here and now.'

'It is not the concert,' said Hedwig sullenly. 'I just don't like to be told to do something without even being asked if I want to do it. And when it comes to it, we are all false and affected, Rudy and Ali and I, we were brought up like this from the beginning because we always had to do things which we never wanted to do and so how could we be otherwise?'

'You are really being childish, Hedwig, and I take this as your excuse. We all have to do things in life which we don't like doing. Surely you don't think that children should be allowed to run loose and get disobedient and disorderly? Think of all the unhappiness I have spared you by bringing you up in the right way.'

'But why was it the right way? How do I know? How do you know?' said Hedwig with white lips. Her eyes began to show red rims as though she was going to cry. 'Only because you say so. As it happens, I would have preferred to be unhappy, so long as it was my own unhappiness and my own doing.'

'You would have preferred——? Hedwig, you can't be right in your head. I have never heard anything like it.'

She paused.

'Hedwig,' she began again, cautiously, with a hurt expression, and pulled a lace-bordered handkerchief out of her bag, 'I am quite calm. I am not angry. I realise that you don't mean what you are saying. This talk about unhappiness, it does not make sense, you have not seen life yet, you don't know what the world is like.'

'And you do, Mama, don't you?'

'I certainly do. And I also know that if we lose our temper with one person it does not mean that he or she has offended us, but that somebody else has. When one receives a kick from above, one passes it on to those below.' She paused again and passed the handkerchief over her eyes and mouth.

'Hedwig,' she said, and gazed above her daughter's head with a determined air. 'Have you been deceiving me in any way? Is there something which you are hiding from me?'

'What do you mean, Mama?' asked Hedwig quickly. She sat up straight; her pallor was suffused by the blood rushing to her face. Her eyes were uneasy.

'I am sure that you have some reason for your bitterness. I do not think for a moment that you intended to be spiteful to me. I know you better than you do yourself. I must conclude that you have had an upsetting experience – elsewhere. Your father has always been a wonderful husband, but he is an exception among men, believe me. Most men want variety at some time or other, which is, of course, a contradiction to happy marriages. Has Ferdinand – I know I should not think it, but what else is there for me to think?'

To her amazement and relief her daughter broke into laughter. 'Nothing of the sort, Mama.'

'I am glad to hear it, very glad,' answered the Baroness and stored her handkerchief away. Her countenance was slightly disappointed. 'Even so, Hedwig. You should be more careful.'

'In what way, Mama?'

'That maid of yours. She is rather pretty. Do you think it wise? It says do not lead us into temptation.'

'I don't care, Mama.'

'There you go again. You are so reckless. One day you will care and it will be too late.' She closed her bag. 'You should have a manservant to answer the door. Ferdinand said something to that effect the other day. I think I will have a look round for someone suitable for you.' She straightened the diamond hoop on her breast and put her bag under her arm. She added: 'Of course, I never thought there was anything seriously wrong. And there is no reason why there should be. You are settled in a beautiful flat – although I do not quite agree with all the arrangements, as you know. But I think I picked you a very suitable place. And you have the most charming husband anybody could wish for. I would be very grieved indeed if you were not satisfied after all the sheer hard work I did for you. And it was hard work, I must be allowed to say so. If things had been left to you, you would not be sitting here today.'

Hedwig rose and went to the window. The air outside was filled with large, slowly drifting snowflakes and the street and the trees in the Stadtpark were dark and glistening with moisture.

'What are you dreaming about now, Hedwig? Don't you ever listen?'

'It is snowing, Mama.'

'How extraordinary,' said the Baroness and turned towards her daughter.

Hedwig said: 'But it won't stay; it dissolves as soon as it touches the ground.'

'I can't say I am surprised. I told you it was too early in the year.' And the Baroness got up with great dignity. 'As I said, it will not take you longer than a fortnight to get through the lists. And if you have any queries, I shall see you before then, in any case.'

'As you say, Mama. If you insist,' and Hedwig followed her mother into the passage with a smile.

The Baroness walked slowly and carefully down the stairs as the rubber soles of her galoshes were clinging to the carpet and impeded her step. As she descended, she ran a finger alternatively over the crimson cord and the balustrade, but only half-heartedly and with a distracted air.

'If only I knew!' she thought. 'Such extraordinary behaviour does not drop from the blue sky. There must be a reason for it somewhere. If only I knew! These palm trees look terribly neglected. In Bubenc that would not be allowed to happen. Those yellow tips must come off. Hedwig thinks people like her better if she is indulgent. But they don't. They only laugh behind her back. If only I knew. I can't very well speak to the Count' – in her thoughts the Baroness still referred to her son-in-law by his title – 'and in any case, I dare say it has all blown over by now.'

She crossed the round, marble-paved hall, passed the niches on her left, and after having cast a rueful glance at the palms and statues, she entered a narrow, short passage lit by a barred window. In one corner stood a broom, a pail and a scrubbing brush.

'If only Hedwig would take me into her confidence,' she thought. 'It is really sad.' And she moved her shoulders so as to bring the high mink collar closer to her throat.

It was sad. With these and similar thoughts, the Baroness busied herself. Like an insect which gathers and amasses grass blades and twigs to build a hiding-place for itself, so the Baroness tried to invent and collect various reasons which would explain Hedwig's behaviour, so that she could safely hide behind their shelter. Never for one moment did it occur to her that her daughter had intended to hit at herself, or that her complaint about Hedwig's lack of confidence was unjustified. Her active brain did not allow her to see that, on the contrary, Hedwig had taken her into her confidence and that her words had been as outspoken as anyone could wish for. And where a more stupid woman would have known that Hedwig's outcry was the truth and have left the flat mortally offended, the Baroness's cleverness enabled her to misunderstand the whole scene by leading her into the agreeable maze of other peoples' wrongdoings. She halted in front of the low door, on which there was a brass plate bearing the words: Alois Hrdina, Caretaker. She knocked. She waited. She knocked again.

The door was opened and the smell of stale coffee, gravy, unaired rooms and wax polish filled the passage. The Baroness held her chin high and said in her low, commanding voice: 'If I am not mistaken, you are the porter, aren't you? In that case – you know who I am? – I should like to say the following. . . .'

After the front door had closed, Hedwig lingered for a while in the hall. 'Please turn the lights out in the dining-room,' she told the maid. 'And you will see some papers on the table. You can throw them away.'

She went into the smoking-room, looked at her own silver-framed photograph on the desk and ran a finger over the coroneted and initialled writing folder. Then she moved to the fireplace and pressed the bell.

The maid entered with a tray on which she carried a small tablecloth. 'Shall I get your tea, madam?' and she removed a vase from a round, rosewood table with lyre-shaped supports ending in lions' paws and a circle of inlaid bronze leaves on the top. Before Hedwig's marriage it had stood in front of the long mirror in her room on the first floor. The maid spread the cloth.

Hedwig looked out of the window with unseeing eyes. 'I imagine Ali will get the table back. It belongs there in any case and she was so angry when I took it with me.'

She turned round, 'Tell me, Agnes, you did take the papers from the dining-room, didn't you?'

'I did, madam. Good gracious me! shouldn't I have burnt them? I could have sworn madam told me to throw them away.'

'You did quite right, Agnes. I only wanted to make sure. And now you can bring me some tea please, but without milk. I shall have a spoonful of brandy in it. Snow and brandy, it somehow goes well together, doesn't it?'

'I should say so, madam.'

'How long has it been snowing now, do you think?'

'About an hour, madam, a good hour easily.'

'And yet,' remarked Hedwig, 'generally it does not snow till the middle of November.' She seemed pleased.

After she had drunk her tea, Hedwig went into the hall and made a telephone call. Then she rang for the maid again. 'Please, Agnes, will you fetch the brown crocodile suitcase from the attic? It needs repairing. I have been wanting to have it put in order for some time already. And when you have brought it down, see that the car comes round in half an hour. I will take it to the trunk makers myself.'

'In this weather, madam? They'll fetch it, they have got their own car.'

'I have got to do other errands as well. I shall drop it on my way there.'

She returned to the smoking-room and sat down by the desk. For a while she stroked the parchment coloured leather which covered the arm of the chair, and played with a fountain pen. At last she frowned, closed her eyes for an instant and swallowed hard. With careful and yet hasty movements, as though afraid to be surprised by someone during her work, she took a sheet out of the folder, placed a square of blotting paper over the bottom and rested her left hand on it, the way she had been trained by Fräulein Lotte, so as to avoid fingermarks.

After she had finished writing, she slipped the folded sheet into an envelope, lit one of the red wax candles which flanked the silver inkstand, and sealed the letter with the signet which belonged to her husband and which bore his crest: a bird on a bough, quartered by a pyramid of stars.

CHAPTER 25

'IT RATTLES like an old tin kettle. It's out of tune,' said Alexandrine for the hundredth time and for the hundredth time Fräulein Lotte answered: 'It is not out of tune. It has a hard, metallic sound, that's all. Good gracious me, do you think madam your mother would allow you to practise on a bad piano?'

'I would not mind so much for myself,' said Alexandrine, with false humility, 'but think of Mrs. Bodner. It must be terribly embarrassing for her to give me lessons on that Boesendorfer.'

Fräulein Lotte thought: 'As though anybody would mind being embarrassed at the rate of fifty crowns an hour.' But she kept silent and gave Alexandrine a little push between the shoulder blades. The young girl drew her brows together, lowered her head and walked slowly along the bare and grey passage. The weekly battle, with its well-worn exclamations and answers which preceded each piano lesson, was nearing its end. She would not have been any happier had she been allowed to use one of the big Bluethners downstairs in the reception rooms, and she knew it. Yet she had to go on, had to say the words which always came at the end of the revolt: 'If only I could use one of the Bluethners downstairs. Hedwig did and she did not play any better than I do now.'

She spoke the last sentence more slowly than usual and looked intently at Fräulein Lotte's face. Today the phrase seemed to carry a new meaning and she was convinced that she would get a new response as well. The word 'Hedwig' was bound to have this effect. She was right. Instead of saying as usual: 'That's what you think. How could you possibly play better than Hedwig and she eight years older than you? Good gracious me. What next?' the German shook her head with a perplexed air and remarked: 'Ah——Hedy. If I were you I would not mention her to Mrs. Bodner.'

Alexandrine said quickly: 'What do you mean?'

'Well, I just should not say that she has gone away. It's not Mrs. Bodner's business.' And as though to underline the meaning of her words, Fräulein Lotte shook her head so that the long black earrings shot like sinister flashes round her face.

Alexandrine said hopefully: 'But Fräulein, she always asks after Hedwig.'

'Then just say, Hedwig is very well, thank you very much, and then get on with your étude.'

They had arrived at the door of the old day nursery. The sound of footsteps and voices drifted up from the hall downstairs.

'Get along now, Ali,' said Fräulein Lotte and turned her head from side to side. She had suddenly grown restless. 'Get your music out and have it all ready before your teacher comes.' And she opened the door. Then she added: 'I'd better go down and see if they want something.'

'Who, Fräulein?' asked the young girl.

'The Count and your mother, Ali.'

'I did not know he was here.'

'He has just arrived,' said Fräulein Lotte.

'How do you know, Fräulein?'

'Because madam your mother has been expecting him, that's why. In you go now.'

Alexandrine stepped inside, threw herself on the black waxcloth settee and let her legs dangle over its back. Something dreadful had happened in connection with Hedwig. If she thought hard about it she might be able to cry. If she only knew what it was that Hedwig had done, it would make the crying so much easier. She squinted at the piano where she soon would be seated and perhaps her tears running down her face and dripping on to her fingers would mark the keys with grey streaks in the way that infuriated Mrs. Bodner so much. Alexandrine looked at her hands lovingly: she had managed not to wash them for a few hours, and had collected a nice lot of dirt.

As Fräulein Lotte went down the stairs she saw the Baroness and the Count standing by the foot of the balustrade, and as she approached the Count turned quickly and looked up at her with an air of cold amusement and expectancy as though willing to welcome any interruption that providence might send his way. 'The poor gentleman,' she thought, 'pulls himself together and puts on a fine show. A real nobleman, I always said so.' And then, when he turned again to the Baroness and assumed a respectful attitude, the housekeeper felt the sudden joy which underlings invariably experience when their superiors are in a difficult position, and she thought: 'I would not like to be in his shoes.' And while she threw a severe glance at the two maids laden with the Count's coat and hat, who showed a marked inclination to linger, she tried to hear what the Baroness was saying. And although the Baroness's face expressed sorrow, kindness, and dignity, Fräulein Lotte was not at all sure whether her mistress's words were sorrowful, kind, and dignified. There was no telling.

'We shall want tea at four. That will be all, Lotte,' said the Baroness to the housekeeper, and led the way to the small drawing-room. The Count followed. Catching a last glimpse of him, Fräulein Lotte thought that even his back looked dejected. 'A real nobleman, from his fingertips to his toes,' she said to herself, and: 'it's a shame'. But had anyone asked her to explain herself, she would not have been able to say what 'the shame' was; whether she was sorry for the Count because of his matrimonial troubles, or because he was being led away by his mother-in-law in order to be subjected to a painful interview or whether it was because he – a true nobleman – had met with misfortune while mingling with a class of people inferior to him by birth – indeed, it was a difficult question.

Again, as not so many months before, the Baroness Kreslov and the Count sat down on the cherry red satin chairs with the lace-clothed table between them on which stood the blue- and gold-rimmed *bonbonnière*. But this was not an occasion for eating chocolates and the ashtray, previously filled with the crumpled-up silver paper, remained empty this time. Like all great ladies and actresses, the Baroness had a fine sense for creating the right setting for her performances and therefore her fingers never strayed towards the chocolates. On the other hand, a woman with less feeling for effect would have made ample use of the handkerchief in a similar situation. But on this point too, the Baroness took the most convincing line: she preferred to be stunned by grief, turned to stone and therefore tragically dry-eyed.

It was exactly a week ago that she had learnt of Hedwig's action and, to her great annoyance, it was only now for the first time that she was able to speak to her son-in-law alone and at length. On the other hand, she was glad of the delay. It gave her more time for planning her decision or, as she called it, 'what was for the best'. At first she had thought of saying 'to think that a daughter of mine' and so on, but she soon realized that this would be a mistake. After all, Hedwig was her daughter and by acknowledging that her daughter had done wrong, she, the mother, would put herself in the wrong too. Then it occurred to her that the best way to make the Count do 'what was for the best' would be to reproach him for his wife's lapse. She would prove to him that he was guilty of neglect and this would put her in a strong position and enable her to impose her terms. Her terms? If someone had been taken into the Baroness's confidence he would have been astonished at the sort of thoughts which rolled through her brain. And, indeed, she had prepared herself for this talk not so much like a grief-stricken mother, but like a business man out to strike a bargain, and who is confident that his experience and his foresight will overcome disaster.

After taking a chair, the Baroness stroked her untidy grey hair and then rested her fingers on the diamond hoop on her breast as though to remind herself by touching this symbol of wealth that everything can be bought at a price and that therefore she need not despair. She cleared her throat, stared at the Count across the table and remained silent. However, if he was disconcerted by her silence, he did not show it. He did not even seem particularly serious and there was a look of patronizing joviality in his face which she did not like at all. At last he said good-naturedly: 'I saw our friend Herring off today, Mama. I gave him all the parcels for Rudy and he will write as soon as he gets to London.' All this he brought out lightly and easily as though to say: 'You see how nice and pleasant I am. If you don't want to talk business, you needn't.'

'Yes, Rudy——' said the Baroness absent-mindedly. 'The dear, good boy.' She closed her eyes for a moment. 'At least he is in good hands in London. The English are nothing if not reliable.' And she opened her eyes and gave the Count another wide, reproachful stare.

'Just so, dear Mama.' And the Count crossed one elegant leg over the other and returned her glance with impeccable composure as though he were well able to praise others for being reliable without any misgivings, as he – Count Szalay – was reliable too. He then asked for permission to smoke and lit a cigarette. 'I need cigarettes now more than ever – my nerves – you understand, dear Mama. You are always so understanding.'

But to judge from his calm and placid countenance, he might have said: 'I now enjoy my cigarettes more than ever, dear Mama. I have not felt so much at my ease for a long, long time.'

They continued silent.

As it was, all the genuine dejection which the Count had experienced on his way to Bubenc had vanished already. The very reluctance of the Baroness to embark on the stormy sea of discussion, was an indication to him that she somehow felt at a disadvantage. Thus reassured, he waited for her to proceed.

'And talking about Rudy and travelling,' began the Baroness and gave him a look meant to be charged with tragic significance, 'I made enquiries at Schencker & Co. and they say that Hedwig bought tickets for the Orient express; to Paris, they say.' She paused. 'Two tickets, Ferdinand. What do you say to that?'

'I don't doubt it, dear Mama. For one thing, I should never doubt anything you tell me and for another, the poor man in question cannot be expected to run after the train all the way from Prague to Paris.'

'You are pleased to joke. Poor man. Is that how you feel about him? I should have thought——'

'You misunderstand me, Mama.' And the Count leaned forward as though eager to amend his mistake. 'I did not say poor because I pity him but because I consider him to be so utterly wretched and wormlike that I cannot even do him the honour of calling him a cad.'

'You are quite right, Ferdinand. I understand you – believe me – only too well,' replied the Baroness with a sigh of relief. And she was really very relieved to find that the Count felt the appropriate emotions of indignation and disgust for the man who had run away with his wife.

On the other hand, the Count was perfectly sincere when he expressed his contempt for the dancer. He felt for him the contempt of the large dog for the small dog and, like the big business man who makes thousands by a single deal and despises the small shopkeeper who earns pennies by continuous and painstaking work, so the Count looked down at the dancer as his inferior in the same profession.

'I should like to have your opinion, Ferdinand. What do you think would be the best course to take?'

'I really don't know, dear Mama. I am still completely broken by the shock. I have not been able to think properly ever since that fatal day.'

'Yes, yes,' said the Baroness impatiently. 'Of course. That's natural. At the moment there is nothing to be done, in any case. We don't know her whereabouts yet; as soon as we find out we can get in touch with her – she will see reason sooner or later, believe me – I don't doubt it for a minute, Ferdinand – you can rest assured of that – I don't doubt it for a minute.' And the Baroness, realizing that she was repeating herself in her eagerness to convince the Count that Hedwig would soon come to heel again, stopped abruptly and assumed a kindly and motherly expression.

'She may and she may not. It is difficult to say,' replied the Count. 'It mainly depends on the working methods of her – eh – companion. If she were on her own, her jewellery, as it is, would last her for years. Still, that's extremely unlikely in the circumstances.'

'But surely you could tell by the tone of her letter what she intended to do?' asked the Baroness and she added with a tone of genuine annoyance: 'If you had only kept the letter, instead of tearing it up. If only I could have had a glance at it. I would have known at once how much of it she meant and how much was sheer rashness. I would not be a mother if I could not tell. Really, Ferdinand, it was most thoughtless of you to destroy the letter, I must be allowed to say so.'

'I deeply regret it myself, dear Mama. But the shock, my nerves, I completely lost my head, you understand,' replied the Count with a quiet smile. As it was, he was most grateful to his wife for having written that letter.

'But what did it say? You must be able to remember some of the words?'

The Count laid a hand on his forehead and drew his brows together. His memory was one of his most valuable assets and, needless to say, he knew the letter by heart; and reviewing the contents quickly, he decided that only one sentence was fit to be communicated to the Baroness. He said hesitantly: 'I seem to remember something like, "You can tell my mother that I shall never return, how you tell her is entirely up to you." That's all, I am afraid. In the beginning of course, there was something about George, that she was going away with him or something in that vein.' And the Count gave his peculiar smile, as though smiling at something inside himself. Hedwig had behaved very decently, there was no denying it. It confirmed again what he had always known – that it paid to be on good terms with women. 'I shall never give you away as long as I live' and she had even underlined it. No, there was nothing to complain about.

After a while, he grew more serious again and straightening his back and smoothing the black ribbon of ribbed silk which was fastened to his eyeglass, he said: 'But in any case, dear Mama, all these are idle speculations. Farewell for ever, can mean a week or months or years. It does not really interest me.'

'It doesn't interest you? Ferdinand, you cannot possibly know what you are saying. I am making allowances for your condition, of course. You are very hurt. And so am I. But although I am deeply wounded by Hedwig's behaviour, I am thinking ahead nevertheless, and I must urge you to do the same. After all, you have been in the war, you have seen life – you know that circumstances change.'

'What you say is very true, dear Mama. You always put things so admirably. Yes, I have seen life. But this sort of thing has never happened to me before, *ça va sans dire*.' And the Count put his head in his hands with a slight but noticeable shudder.

Again, the Baroness showed signs of impatience. 'I agree, Ferdinand. It is a disaster.'

'It is more than that, dear Mama. It is a scandal. Disaster is one thing, scandal another.'

The Baroness straightened her back and sat very upright. 'It is you who have said it. Not I. It need not be a scandal. It must not be.'

'Is that so?'

'Yes, that is so. As I see it, it is your duty to fetch Hedwig back from Paris. After all, in a way, it is your fault that all this has happened, you will allow me to say so. If you had been more careful and more on the look-out, the whole thing could have been prevented.'

'How true, dear Mama. But as it was, it never occurred to me that a girl like Hedwig, so carefully brought up, could have acted in this way. Brought up in a house like yours, dear Mama.'

'I have always done my duty by Hedwig.'

'So have I,' said the Count. 'I think I can say that I have been an attentive and considerate husband.' He fell silent and raised a questioning glance at his mother-in-law, like a player who has delivered his stroke and wonders in what manner his opponent is going to return the ball.

To her dismay, the Baroness realized that they had come to a deadlock and that she had to start from a different angle. 'For your own sake, Ferdinand,' she began, 'I should think it essential that you get Hedwig back as soon as you can. Your position in this town – you have already made a great number of friends – are you going to admit to them that you were not able to keep your own wife in order?'

The Count shrugged and gave her a melancholy look.

'Unfortunately I have become a fatalist during the last few years. And then, I don't pretend to be perfect. My friends will have to make their minds up whether to drop me or not.'

'You mean that you are willing to continue in Prague, without Hedwig, with the scandal of a broken marriage hanging over your head and expecting Franz and myself to live it down?'

The Count said humbly: 'I don't see what else there is for me to do, dear Mama.'

'But I am telling you the whole time, Ferdinand. If you would only listen. You must take her back.'

'Haha!' said the Count. 'That is rich! That is priceless! Forgive my amusement, dear Mama, at this untimely moment, but you seem to have misunderstood me completely.'

With a violent jerk, he pushed his chair away from the table, got up and paced several times up and down the room, while the Baroness followed his movements with a martyr's glances and with her hands acrossed above her breast, as though to convince an invisible audience that she was being forced to suffer the greatest indignities.

At last he came to a standstill in front of the harpsichord, propped himself up on his elbows, crossed one foot over the other with a show of impertinence and elegance, and said: 'Thank God I am not a snob, dear Mama, because if I were, I would already have walked out of here. And therefore it is very painful to me that I have to remind you' – and he raised one hand and contemplated his trim finger-nails – 'that I am not a greengrocer or a—a—timber merchant, but that I am a Szalay. Of course, I won't pretend that our family has been exempt from that sort of occurrence – a coronet is not a shield against fate. Indeed, I often think it invites and attracts the cruelties of fate. Ah, when I think of it. My father, my mother, my brothers, the estate, and now this. This! Irretrievable, like all the rest.' And continuing in the contemplation of his finger-nails, the Count continued to murmur words which were almost inaudible. The Baroness fancied that 'Fate' and 'Coronet' and 'Blue Blood' occurred several times and the longer it went on, the greater her exasperation became. Already she realized that she had no means of forcing her son-in-law to take Hedwig back and that she would have to save the situation in a less satisfactory manner, although she did not yet see how.

As soon as he felt that his mother-in-law was deprived of most of her fighting spirit, the Count ceased his muttering and put a on good show of the man who could go on for hours, but decides to pull himself together.

'As I said, dear Mama, the situation is not entirely unknown to my family. In former times we used to deal with it accordingly, we killed the women or exiled them. Those were the so-called barbaric days. So-called, I say, because personally I don't find those methods so very unreasonable. However, I shall spare your feelings. But barbaric or not, never has a Szalay been known to forgive an unfaithful wife. And when I say never, I cover a long time, dear Mama. And I should like to remind you that one of my ancestors was already present at the coronation of Saint Stephen in the eleventh century, although we were not Counts then, only Barons. And nobody can rob me of this feeling, this knowledge. You may find it hard to understand, dear Mama, but there it is. I may be an officer without a regiment, a landed gentleman without an estate, a subject of a kingdom without a king, but I still am a Szalay.'

'My God! Of course. I never said a word to the contrary, dear Ferdinand. There is no need to get so *échauffé*,' said the Baroness.

'Isn't there,' replied the Count grimly and sat down. He felt he deserved a rest.

He fell silent, his head in his hands and gave a sigh from time to time.

The Baroness, too, was silent and sat very still, but her breath could be heard in the stillness: heavy, trembling and irregular. 'I shall not let him go until something is settled,' she kept saying to herself. 'I cannot possibly leave it to Franz. As I know him, he would pull out his cheque-book and start to bargain. He has no idea how to treat a man of breeding and sensibility. Thank God I am here. If Franz had had this conversation, the Count would have left a long time ago. If this is not hushed up, I shall die. Yes, I shall die and they will bury me.' And although she had never felt less willing to die, although she was planning ahead and trying to shape the future, the Baroness repeated these tragically voluptuous sentences in her mind, and gradually grew calmer. She cleared her throat.

'In the meantime,' she said, 'I have talked to Franz and my brother Richard, and we have agreed that for the time being the best thing to say is that Hedwig has gone to Vienna to stay with friends. Do you agree to that, Ferdinand?'

'Certainly, dear Mama. If you feel that it will help you to give out this story, I shall not stand in your way and, really, I want to give you all the help I can in this – scandalous affair. That is, you understand, as long as you do not demand the impossible from me. But I am sure you won't. You have always understood me so well.'

'I am glad to hear you say so,' replied the Baroness and gave him a kind look. She felt that somehow the worst of the talk was over. The climate of the conversation had changed from 'stormy' and 'cloudy' to 'calm' and 'wind-still'.

She continued slowly and warily, ready to stop as soon as the Count would show any sign of 'getting out of hand' as she put it.

'But this, as I need hardly point out, is only for the time being. Hedwig can stay away for a fortnight, for three weeks, perhaps for a month, but not longer. People will ask for her address, will want to look her up, take messages and so on. It is not a solution to our difficulties.'

'Is there ever any solution to anybody's difficulties?' asked the Count and turned to the harpsichord as though addressing that instrument. 'Take me, for instance, dear Mama. Here I am, I will not speak about myself as I see myself, but as you see me. Here I am then, an embarrassment to you and the Baron, by my sheer presence. No, please, don't protest. I know it only too well. And as I said already a minute ago, I would be only too glad to be of assistance to you. And not only this, I know where the right course lies for me. And yet, how am I to follow it?' And he continued to gaze at the harpsichord.

'What do you mean, Ferdinand?'

'Nothing much, dear Mama. An idea not worth talking about. What good are ideas if we cannot put them into being?'

'Please tell me, Ferdinand.'

It was always the Count's rule never to demand a thing, but to arrange it in such a way that it would be pressed upon him. He felt that the talk was going in the right direction and therefore he consented to reveal his 'idea'.

He said: 'I should go away. I should disappear. That would be the only thing to do. With both of us out of the way, and nobody to contradict you, you could then say that Hedwig and I have gone to Hungary to settle at the family place. Family place! Ha!' And the Count shrugged.

'But this is an excellent idea!' exclaimed the Baroness. 'No, wait, it is not impossible. It can be done quite easily. Franz could find you a position anywhere. In London, Paris, South America. Wherever you wish. We are – as you know – quite well connected.'

'It sounds very nice, dear Mama,' replied the Count with a downhearted smile.

'It is very nice, Ferdinand.'

'It is as nice and plausible as all impossible projects, dear Mama. Do you really think that I am going to finish my life sitting on an office stool and getting a shine on the seat of my trousers?'

'If I may say so, you are being absurd,' said the Baroness. 'What else have you been doing the last few months? You went to Heuwagsplatz day in, day out, and you liked it. At least, you gave that impression. Is it possible that you have been deceiving us?'

'Not at all,' said the Count and rose again and took up his wanderings up and down the Aubusson carpet, from one end of its flowered border to the other. 'Then I had something – I mean someone – to work for. But now? No. I am afraid this is quite impossible.'

'My God, Ferdinand,' replied the Baroness, 'why should it be impossible?' And she added: 'You are making it so very difficult for me. Yes, really you are.' This she said in the tone of voice which one uses to scold a dog who has misbehaved, and she did not expect an answer from her son-in-law any more than one would expect it from a dog.

The Count lowered his head and stared at the flowers woven into the carpet, curling over the ground which had the pallid green colour of a sickly lawn on a frosty morning.

At four o'clock, when the footman came in with the tea equipage, he found the Count seated by the small table and gazing into the distance with a vague smile, while the Baroness stood by one of the windows, tugging at a tasselled cord. Her hair was so untidy that it looked almost dishevelled and her face and throat were flushed. She seemed exhausted and displeased.

'Come and draw the curtains,' she ordered the footman. 'One of the rings has got stuck on the runners. It seems I am expected to look after everything.'

But before the footman was able to attend to her command, she told him to leave the room.

When the Baron Kreslov came home that night, he did not even greet his wife, but said straight away: 'Well, Melanie, did you see him?'

The Baroness nodded.

'How much?' asked the Baron.

'You are revolting, Franz. Because you think of nothing but money, you think everyone else does, too.'

'And so they do, Melanie.'

The Baroness ignored this and continued: 'You may thank God that I saw him. At least I know how to handle people, which is more than you do. Your coarseness would have disgusted the Count. Fortunately, I happen to understand him.' And she closed her eyes for an instant.

'Glad to hear it, Melanie. Now for heaven's sake, let's have it, just to pacify my coarse nature – one million crowns or two?'

'Three, Franz.' And the Baroness left the room and closed the door softly behind her, self-possessed to the last.

CHAPTER 26

IT WAS half-past three in the afternoon. The November sun shone with frosty and diamantine clearness through the dusty curtains of Richard Marek's library and revealed brownish streaks on the green velvet hangings, where the pile had worn off. Two of the gilded sphinxes, which supported the top of the writing table, reflected the light on their coldly magnificent faces, melancholy symbols of Napoleonic glory.

Rollo lay by the stove in the corner with his head on his front paws, pretending to sleep. From time to time, he opened his eyes and, too lazy to lift his head, he rolled them towards his master in order to observe him.

Richard Marek paced up and down the floor, cigarette in hand, leaving a trail of ashes behind him on the carpet. Steffanie Smejkal was leaning comfortably in one of the red armchairs and contemplated the dog at her feet. She held her hat and grey astrakhan muff on her knees. Above the rough grey wintry curls of the astrakhan collar, her face looked worn and delicate.

'Really, Steffie,' said Richard Marek without stopping in his exercise. 'I understand you. I always understand you, that goes without saying. But even so – *tout comprendre* is not always *tout pardonner*. If you knew Hedwig was up to no good, why didn't you speak up?'

He raised his arm as though to guard against her interrupting him, although she gave no sign to do so. 'I know. You don't have to tell me. You thought it was amusing and you settled back in your seat to enjoy the circus. Besides, you never liked Ferdinand.'

'I never did, I never shall, Richard. But then – have a heart. How was I to know that she would run away. An affair is one thing and leaving your husband another. And if every woman walked out on her husband when she had an affair, there would be no marriages left. You know that as well as I do.'

'Ha.'

'So what was I to do? Go to the manager of the Elysée and tell him to sack that Bobby or George or whatever his name is? Or go to Melanie? I would not have come home alive.'

'I suppose you would not.'

'Or go to the Count disguised as his best friend? I hate to say this, but I think you ought to know? And tell him to defend his wife's honour? Don't be ridiculous, Richard. He must have known all the time.'

'Do you think so?' asked Richard Marek, stroking his hair and looking dubious.

'I am convinced of it. And he probably thought the same as I, that it would blow over, and did not trouble any further.'

'In that case, he is a fool.'

'No, Richard. A woman can always defend herself and if she cannot, it means that she does not want to. Besides, what was he to defend? I am not so sure that Hedwig had an affair at all.'

'Not at all?'

'I should not be surprised. Still, in the end it comes to the same,' and Steffanie crossed her legs with a pretty movement and smiled politely at her friend.

Richard Marek came and sat down on a chair beside her. Rollo crawled up to him and put his head over his master's feet.

'Get up, curse you!' exclaimed Richard Marek and shook him off. 'I am already hot enough as it is.' The dog rose with an offended air and slunk behind the settee.

'Now, now, Richard, come, come. I thought you only kicked the dog when Melanie was about.'

'So I do. I was just thinking of her.'

'So was I, Richard. It is difficult not to.'

He lit a cigarette with a worried air. 'If Hedwig had only written some sort of letter to Melanie as well. Melanie can't get over it. And Ferdinand won't show his.'

'He probably knows why.'

'Probably,' replied Richard Marek and stared ahead of him; he looked preoccupied.

'You know, Steffie, that's the queer thing about this whole to-do. I think of Melanie the whole time. And yet, strictly speaking, I should be thinking of Ferdinand. After all, he is the husband. It is he who has been wronged, if you will forgive this big word. At least, that is how it should be, but it isn't. He does not behave as though he had been wronged at all; wronged in his feelings, if you know what I mean. He behaves as though he's backed the wrong horse at a race meeting, or something of the sort. Too gentlemanly for words. Damn the nobility. So there he sits on his blue-blooded bottom and gives that smile of his – you know, he always smiles in that way. And all the time Melanie does the real work, tries to find out where Hedwig has got to and follows it up. When I come to think of it, it is Melanie who behaves the way the husband should. Or do you think that's just my imagination?'

'Not at all.'

'She is a beastly, interfering old woman, but she sees a thing through. She has her points after all.'

'Naturally, Richard. You say that as though it surprised you. And as we have got so far already, I will tell you something more. Melanie behaves just as she should, because she is the wronged party and nobody else. Hedwig did not run away because she had enough of her Count – that's incidental. I don't care to whom you are married – once you have lived with a man for a year, you feel like kicking him down the back stairs. That's nothing. Hedwig ran away to spite her mother, I am absolutely sure of it. And the only way to make Hedwig come back is to do away with Melanie, and in that regard Hedwig is not alone. And now you know why I never said a word before. It would have led to nothing.'

'So that's it,' said Richard Marek. 'Women are peculiar.'

'Are they, Richard? And what about yourself? When you married Sophy, you talked of decency and doing one's duty, and you were kind, because men who marry beneath themselves are always kind. But wasn't there more to it as well? It was your way of kicking Melanie, be sincere about it.'

'May be. I won't contradict you, Steffie. But why shouldn't I have married Sophy? I was free to do as I pleased. And I did it and nobody could stop me. It just showed Melanie.'

'Exactly. You had to prove to Melanie how free you were. But a free man does not have to prove his freedom. It is only when you are not, that you have to do so. And now I must go. I have told you enough home-truths for one afternoon and I have to go home and dispense tea. But before I leave, tell me, Richard, what shall I say when anybody enquires? What is Melanie's official version?'

'Hedwig has gone to Vienna to stay with friends.'

'Vienna it shall be.'

They got up and went downstairs, followed by Rollo, who sat down beneath the hall table in a most uncomfortable position, as he had to squeeze himself between the three marble women who supported the top with their interlaced arms; from there he displayed his noble and dejected profile.

Joseph came out from the passage and remained standing by the foot of the stairs.

'Good bye, Richard. And be kind to the dog.'

'If you say so. I kiss your hand, Steffie.'

After he had closed the front door, Richard Marek turned to the servant: 'What are you mooning about for, like a sheep when it thunders? What's the use of standing about? Either you don't come out at all, but if you do, then open the door for Mrs. Smejkal or do something useful. Or do you think you are such a pretty sight that it is just enough if you show your nose?'

'I thought you'd prefer to show Madam out yourself, sir.'

'You break my heart, Joseph. I'll tell you why you came out. You wanted to listen.'

'At your service, sir.'

'But you didn't hear anything, did you?'

'No, sir,' and Joseph distended his nostrils and pressed his hands to the seams of his shabby trousers.

'And you won't hear anything either, Joseph. Because there is nothing to hear. And when Miss Hedwig comes back from Vienna, we'll clear the house up and give a party. The house is a pigsty, but that does not mean that it is going to stay that way.'

'No, sir.'

Joseph returned to the kitchen which was filled with steam. The bare acacia tree in the yard outside showed through the dimmed window-pane and beyond it rose the tiers of slatternly balconies, festooned with their perennial vegetation of rags, and planted with brooms and broken flower-pots.

'What's up now?' asked the cook and stirred the contents of a pan on the stove with ill restrained brutality.

'Nothing, just the same.'

'It's a pity.'

'No, it isn't. Serves them right.'

CHAPTER 27

'WELL, if you insist, my dear Count.'

'I do, Professor. You will agree that your picture is much too good to be dragged about in hotel rooms and go mouldy in the end in some God-forsaken attic.'

Professor Surovy was sitting in an armchair in front of the fireplace in the smoking-room. The logs were almost burnt down to white and shivering ashes and in their dying flame the pale marble hearth was dipped into a faint red glow.

The Count sat on the desk with his feet resting on a stool.

The painting of the Slovak peasant girls was propped up against one of the bookcases. He inhaled the smoke of his cigarette deeply and blew rings into the air with an expression of satisfied virtuosity.

'Prague is a charming town,' he continued, 'but charm is not enough. Nobody knows that better than I do. After all, I always have been a rolling stone and a rolling stone I shall remain. My country has been overrun by the Turks in the past and we have taken over fatalism from them. It was fate, Professor. Hedwig was not unfaithful to me.'

'My dear Count. I appreciate your chivalry.'

'I don't bother to be chivalrous. It is the truth.'

'If you say so, dear Count,' and the old man adjusted his

238

gold-rimmed pince-nez with an elegant and deliberate movement, as though he had been examining an *objet d'art* and had formed his judgment on it.

'It is I who have been unfaithful. Not in the way you mean. Unfaithful to myself. I should have remained what I was instead of settling down. And I believe Hedwig felt the same.'

'Who is to say, dear Count?'

'Fate is like my esteemed mother-in-law, Professor. She always wants to have the last word. When one is destined to be hanged, one does not die by drowning. That is a manner of speech of course, but you see what I mean.'

'We shall all be very sorry to lose you, dear Count, I can sincerely assure you of that. But I understand, and sympathise with you in your loss.'

'Yes, I suppose it was a loss. I can't say I have gained much. Except that my wardrobe is in a much better condition than it was before.'

'I admire your sense of humour, dear Count.'

'Not at all, Professor. Clothes are very important, don't you think?'

'Everything is important, dear Count.'

FINIS

THE HOGARTH PRESS

This is a paperback list for today's readers – but it holds to a tradition of adventurous and original publishing set by Leonard and Virginia Woolf when they founded The Hogarth Press in 1917 and started their first paperback series in 1924.

Some of the books are light-hearted, some serious, and include Fiction, Lives and Letters, Travel, Critics, Poetry, History and Hogarth Crime and Gaslight Crime.

A list of our books already published, together with some of our forthcoming titles, follows. If you would like more information about Hogarth Press books, write to us for a catalogue:

40 William IV Street, London WC2N 4DF

Please send a large stamped addressed envelope

HOGARTH FICTION

Behind A Mask: The Unknown Thrillers of Louisa May Alcott
Edited and Introduced by Madeleine Stern

Death of a Hero by Richard Aldington
New Introduction by Christopher Ridgway

The Amazing Test Match Crime by Adrian Alington
New Introduction by Brian Johnston

Epitaph of a Small Winner by Machado de Assis
Translated and Introduced by William L. Grossman

Mrs Ames by E.F. Benson
Paying Guests by E.F. Benson
Secret Lives by E.F. Benson
New Introductions by Stephen Pile

Ballantyne's Folly by Claud Cockburn
New Introduction by Andrew Cockburn
Beat the Devil by Claud Cockburn
New Introduction by Alexander Cockburn

Chance by Joseph Conrad
New Introduction by Jane Miller

Lady Into Fox & A Man in the Zoo by David Garnett
New Introduction by Neil Jordan

The Whirlpool by George Gissing
New Introduction by Gillian Tindall

Morte D'Urban by J.F. Powers
Prince of Darkness and other stories by J.F. Powers
New Introductions by Mary Gordon

Mr Weston's Good Wine by T.F. Powys
New Introduction by Ronald Blythe

The Revolution in Tanner's Lane by Mark Rutherford
New Introduction by Claire Tomalin
Catharine Furze by Mark Rutherford
Clara Hopgood by Mark Rutherford
New Afterwords by Claire Tomalin

The Last Man by Mary Shelley
New Introduction by Brian Aldiss

The Island of Desire by Edith Templeton
Summer in the Country by Edith Templeton
New Introductions by Anita Brookner

Christina Alberta's Father by H.G. Wells
Mr Britling Sees It Through by H.G. Wells
New Introductions by Christopher Priest

Frank Burnet by Dorothy Vernon White
New Afterword by Irvin Stock

H.G. Wells

The Wife of Sir Isaac Harman

New Introduction by Victoria Glendinning

The Wife of Sir Isaac Harman, one of the funniest and boldest of Wells's novels, is a lively survey of sex, society and freedom, and all their attendant complications.

Sir Isaac Harman, International Bread and Cake magnate, suffers from determined women: suffragette sisters, striking waitresses, loud-voiced dowagers. Trembling, he locks up his young wife and reads *The Taming of the Shrew*. Too late: Lady Harman picks up a poker and makes her break, watched with devoted eagerness by Mr Brumley, middle-aged writer turned knight-errant – one of Wells's most endearing comic heroes. Can Lady Harman escape him too?

Edith Templeton
The Island of Desire

New Introduction by Anita Brookner

The Island of Desire celebrates erotic love with wit, charm and honesty. It tells the story of Franciska Kalny, daughter of Mrs Kalny, who with her snobbery and her lovers sets the sort of example which requires a daughter to rebel. So Franciska deserts the decadence of Prague and embarks on a voyage of self-discovery through seedy Parisian nightclubs and the haunts of millionaire Americans, chintzy English suburbs and the romantic piazzas of Italy. Her journey is every woman's rite of passage: anarchic, tentative and tragi-comic, it demonstrates an eternal truth – that the loss of innocence is merely the beginning of the dubious rewards that adult love so inevitably brings.

Mark Rutherford
Catharine Furze
New Afterword by Claire Tomalin

Catharine's desires are those of every girl as she grows into womanhood – idealistic, absurd, passionate, barely spoken. In telling her story Mark Rutherford became one of the first male novelists to write sympathetically about the fate of women, and this book, along with *Clara Hopgood*, has been sought after for many years. It is his finest novel: Dickensian in its humour and pathos, exceptional in its understanding of a woman's troubled soul.

Mary Shelley
The Last Man

New Introduction by Brian Aldiss

The fame of *Frankenstein*, Mary Shelley's classic tale, has, over the years, eclipsed the splendour of her other novels. Perhaps the most unjustly neglected of these is *The Last Man*, an apocalyptic vision of love and loss set in a republican England of the twenty-first century and one of the most innovative novels of its time. Against ever-changing landscapes of fast-flowing torrents and vast starry skies, a tiny band of adventurers leave their pastoral idyll for the turmoil of national politics, Mediterranean wars and worldwide catastrophe. With its tender fictional portraits of Byron, Shelley and Claire Clairmont, *The Last Man* is a paean to a lost generation; it is also one of our great Romantic novels.

Compton Mackenzie
Vestal Fire

New Introduction by Sally Beauman

On sublime Sirene, set in the glittering waters of the Salernian Gulf, Miss Virginia and Miss Maimie's enthusiasm for the mysterious but impeccably wealthy Count Marsac is of consuming interest to all. The Count is not only outrageous but incorrigible, however, and soon a catspaw of rumour concerning his past becomes a whirlwind of controversy.

A glorious canvas, painted with Dickensian energy, *Vestal Fire* is based on the characters who lived on Capri at the beginning of this century, such as E.F. Benson and Norman Douglas. But as in all great humour, the book, with its longing for a lost idyll, is ultimately as moving as it is funny.

George Gissing
Will Warburton

New Introduction by John Halperin

Will Warburton, Victorian gentleman, is apparently secure. He has a prestigious job, rosy prospects, a beloved family and many friends. But then disaster strikes, and Will, forced to become a grocer, finds out what his friends are made of . . .

Written while he was dying, this is one of Gissing's finest novels. Will Warburton, with his petty snobberies and all-too-human weaknesses, is a hero unique in Victorian fiction, personifying, as he does, the gnawing fears, comic absurdities and optimistic self-deception that are hallmarks of class prejudice.

Colin MacInnes
All Day Saturday

New Introduction by Tony Gould

Everybody loves Mrs Helen Bailey – everybody, that is, except her husband Walter, who sits alone in the Australian sun, polishing his guns. For Helen, a faded *femme fatale*, destiny seems to hold only embittered passion, infertility and a lifetime of tea parties. But one Saturday a young stranger arrives – and the lives and loves on the Baileys' sheep station are altered forever.

A novel which may surprise those who know Colin MacInnes through *Absolute Beginners*, *All Day Saturday* is, at once, a telling portrait of a troubled marriage, a comic evocation of life in the Bush, and a classical drama – where the fates of many are decreed in a day.